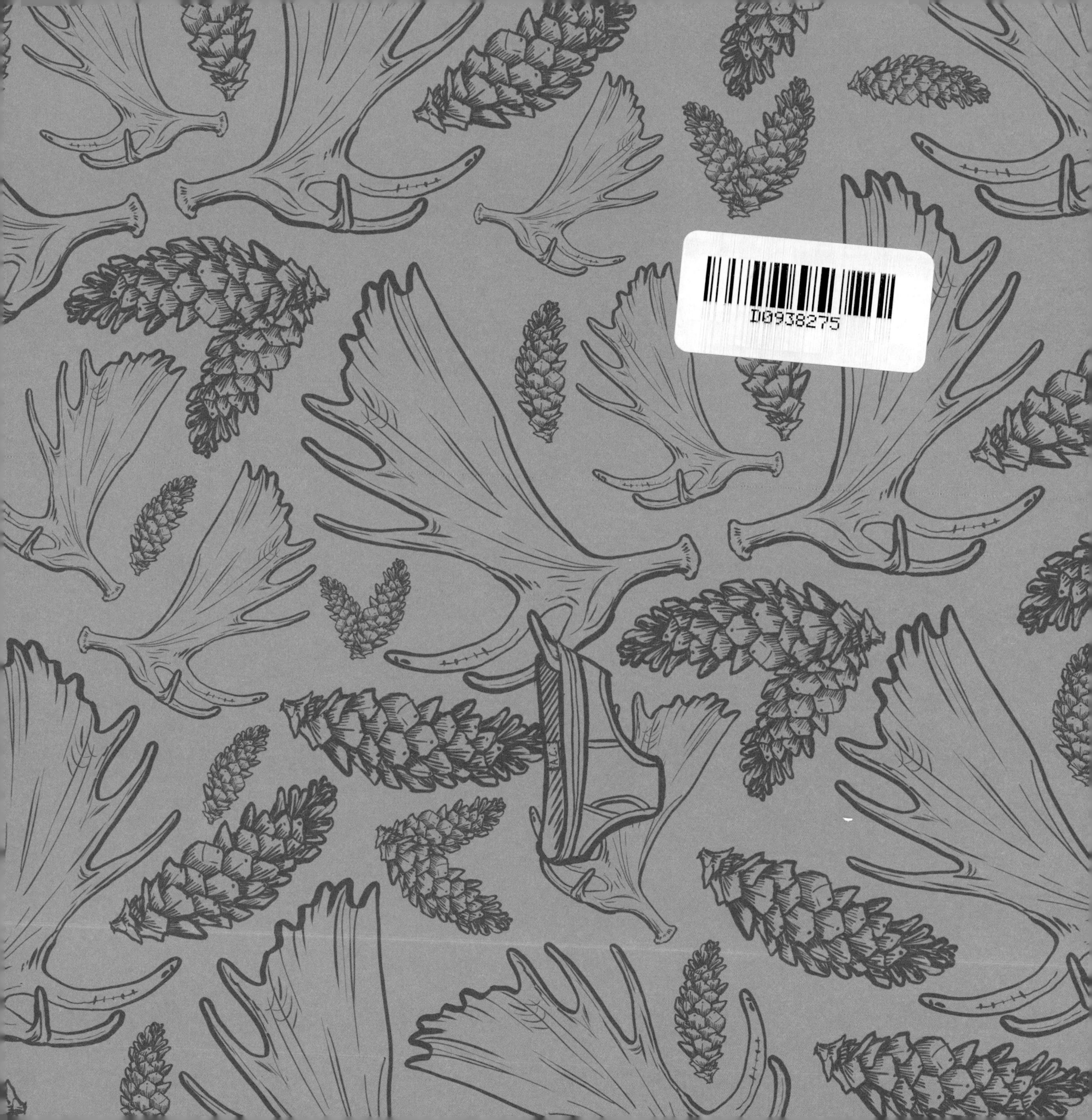

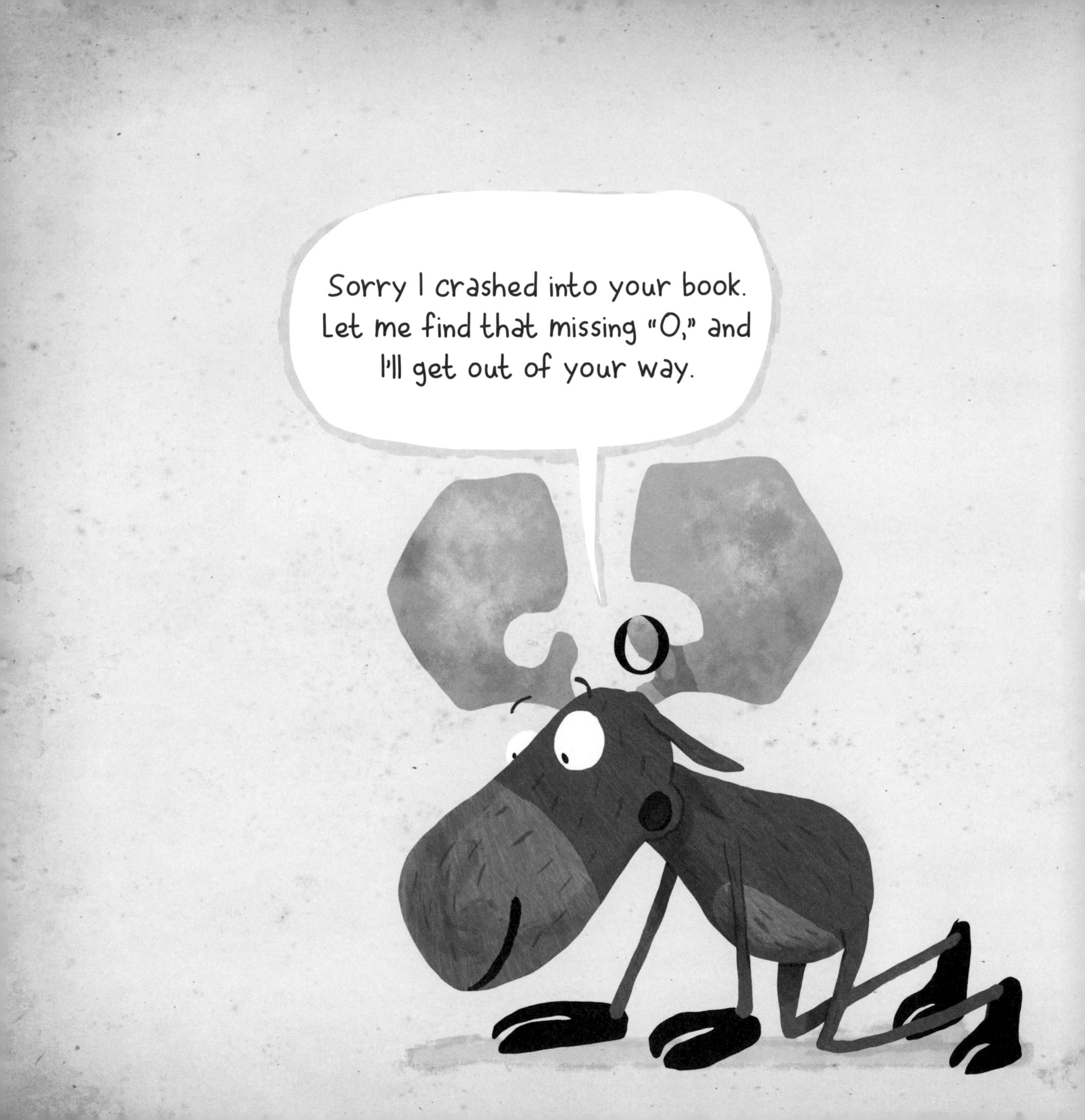
Sorry I crashed into your book. Let me find that missing "O," and I'll get out of your way.
O

This Is a  Whoopsie!

By Andrew Cangelose

Illustrated by Josh Shipley

M o se

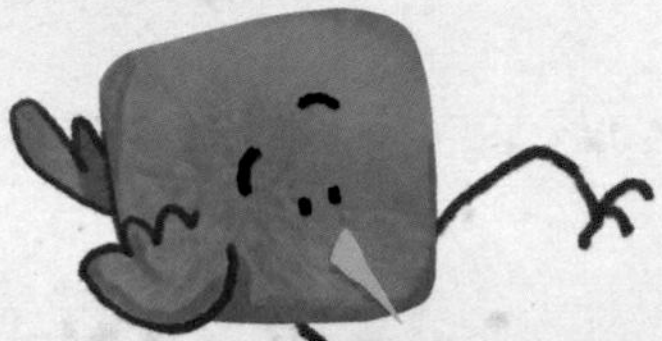

This is a moose.

Hey, I think you're supposed to be here.

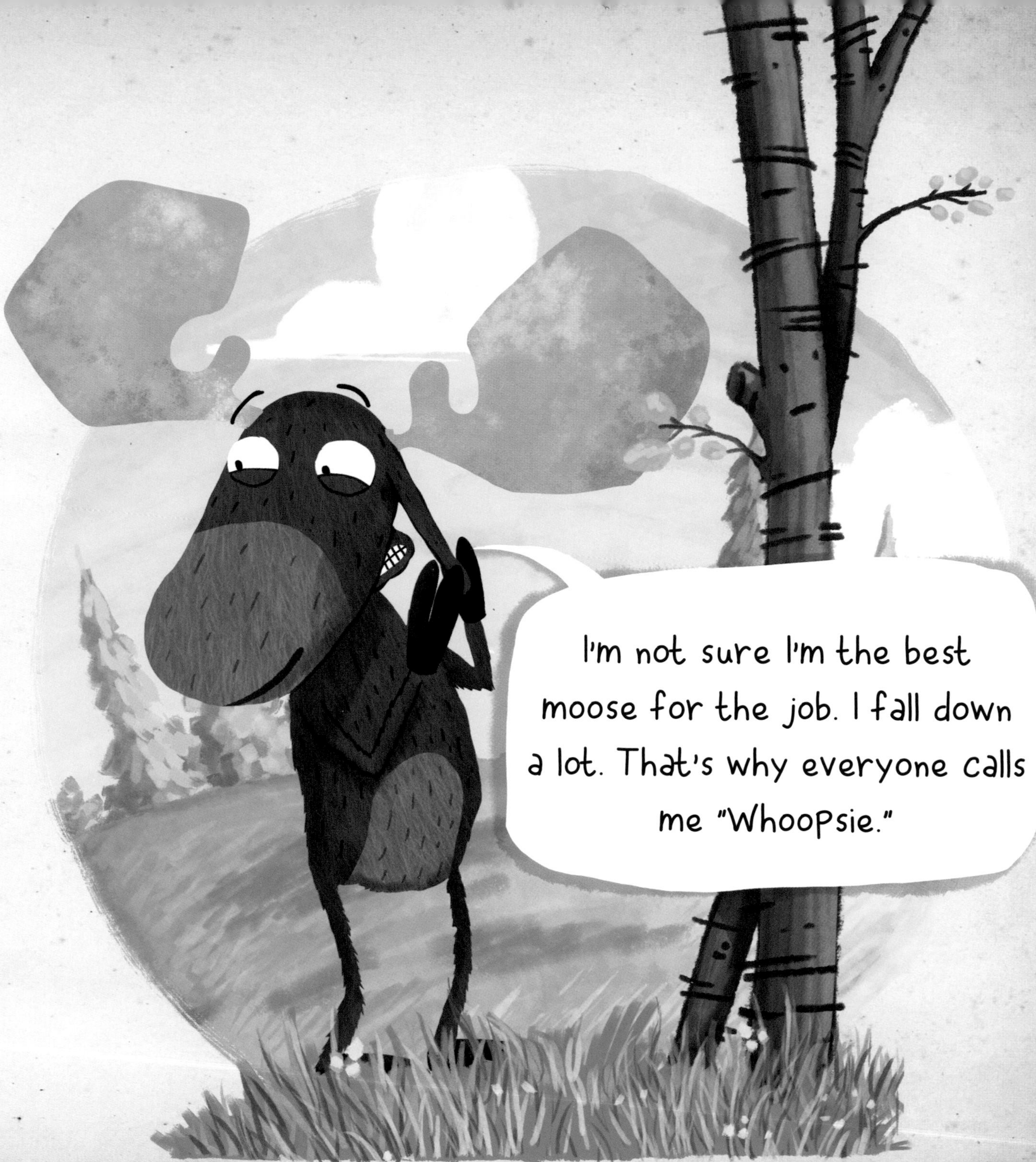
I'm not sure I'm the best moose for the job. I fall down a lot. That's why everyone calls me "Whoopsie."

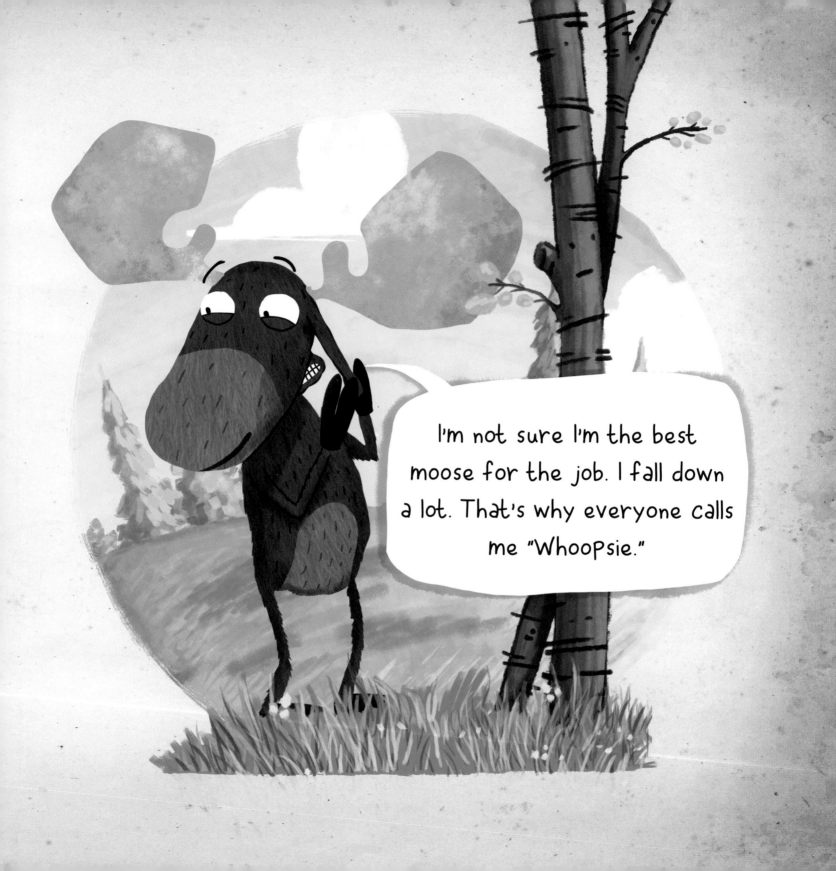

Moose are the tallest mammals in North America. They can grow up to seven feet high. That's taller than most professional basketball players.

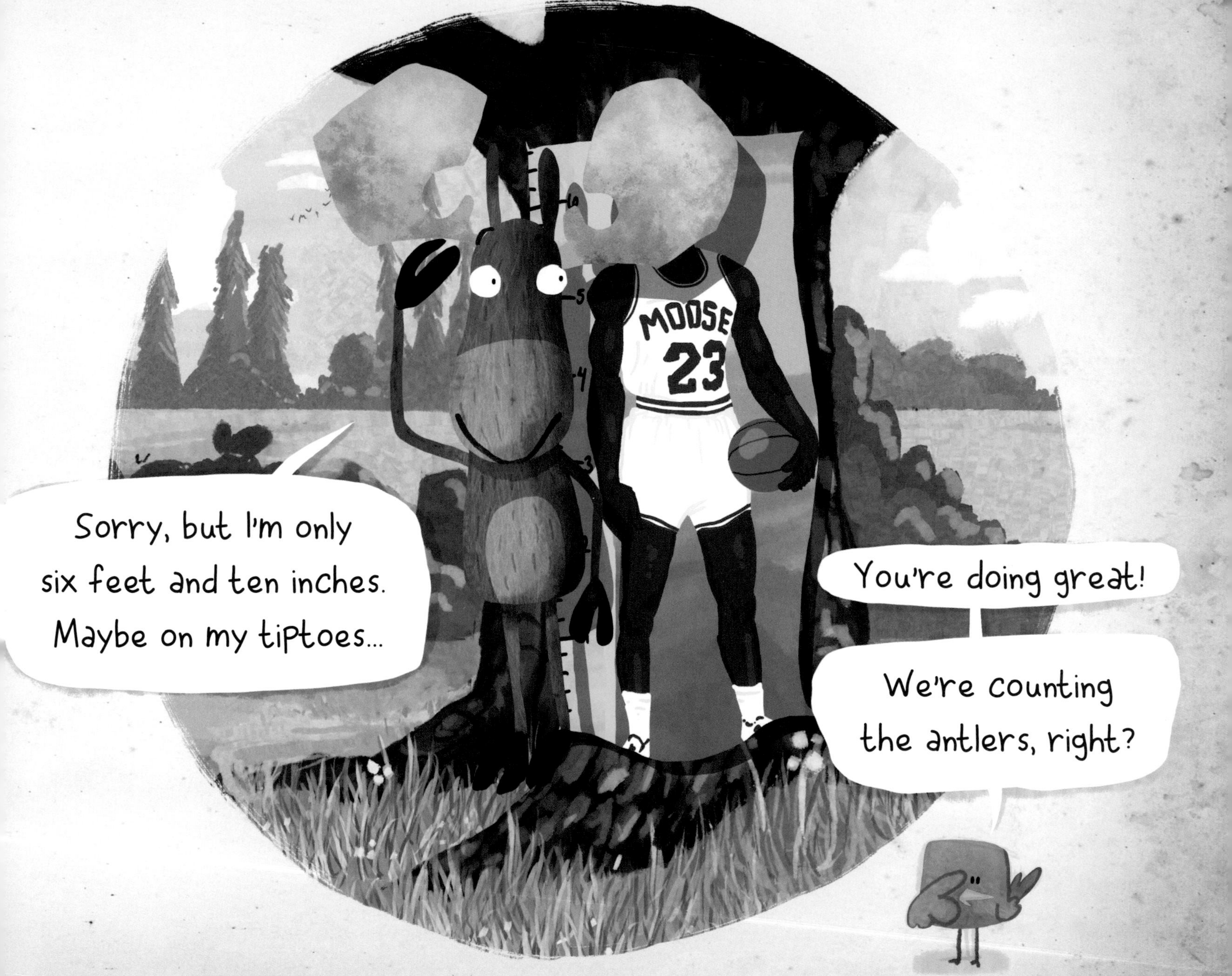

MOOSE
23
Sorry, but I'm only six feet and ten inches. Maybe on my tiptoes...
You're doing great!
We're counting the antlers, right?

The plural of *moose* is *moose*. That means whether it is one moose or many moose, the word is still *moose*.

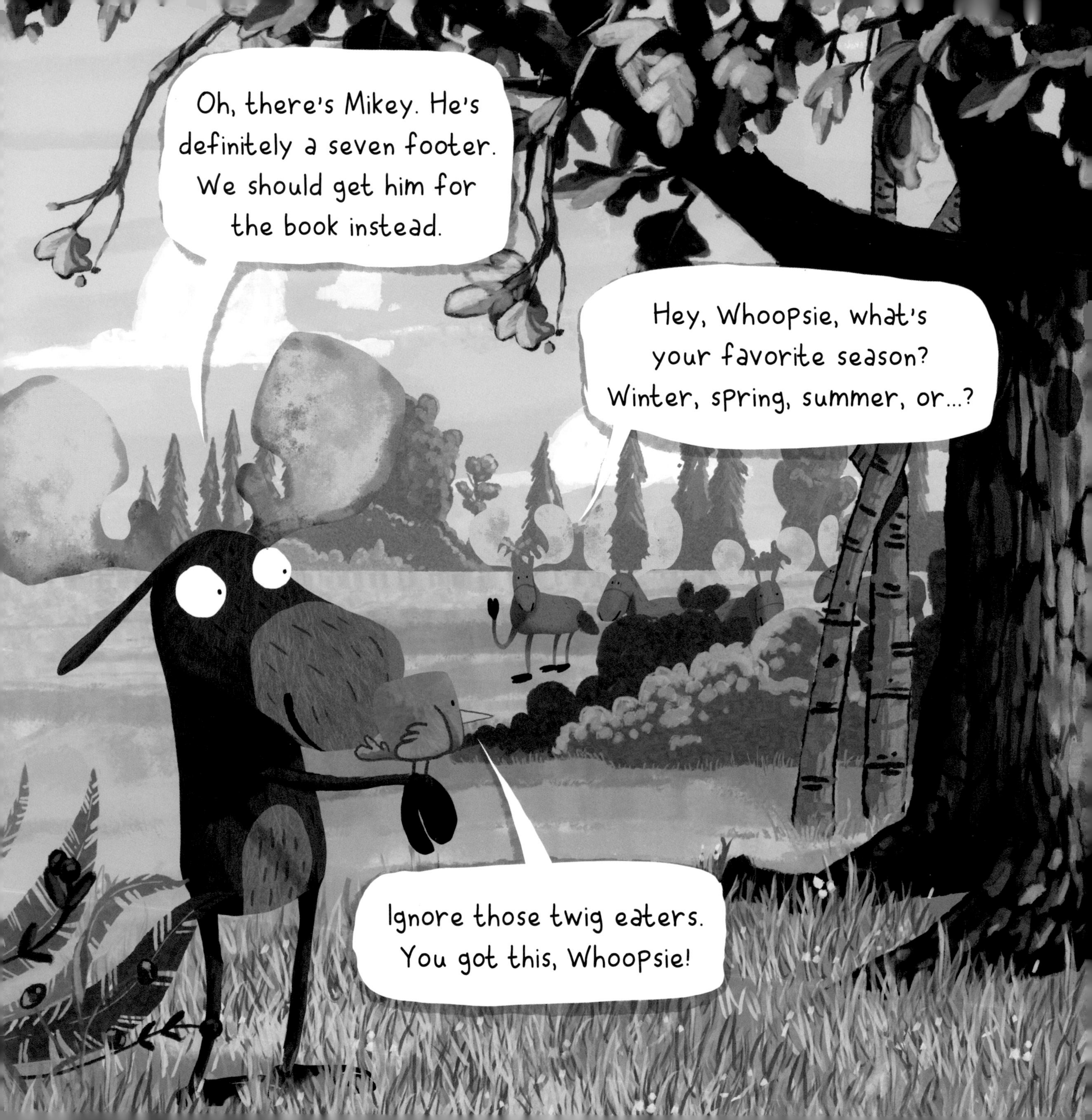
Oh, there's Mikey. He's definitely a seven footer. We should get him for the book instead.
Hey, Whoopsie, what's your favorite season? Winter, spring, summer, or...?
Ignore those twig eaters. You got this, Whoopsie!

A moose can run at speeds of up to 35 miles per hour. That's fast enough to get a speeding ticket in most neighborhoods!

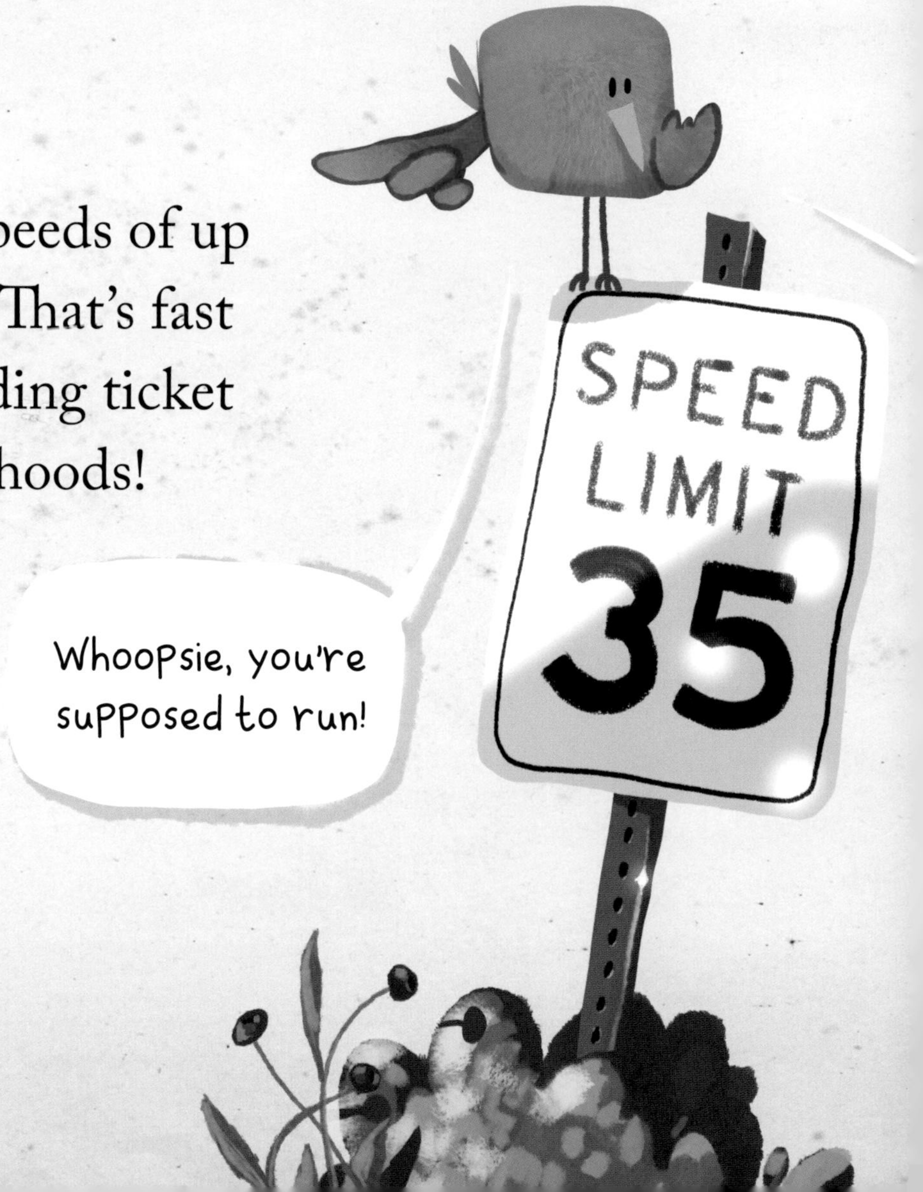
Whoopsie, you're supposed to run!
SPEED LIMIT 35

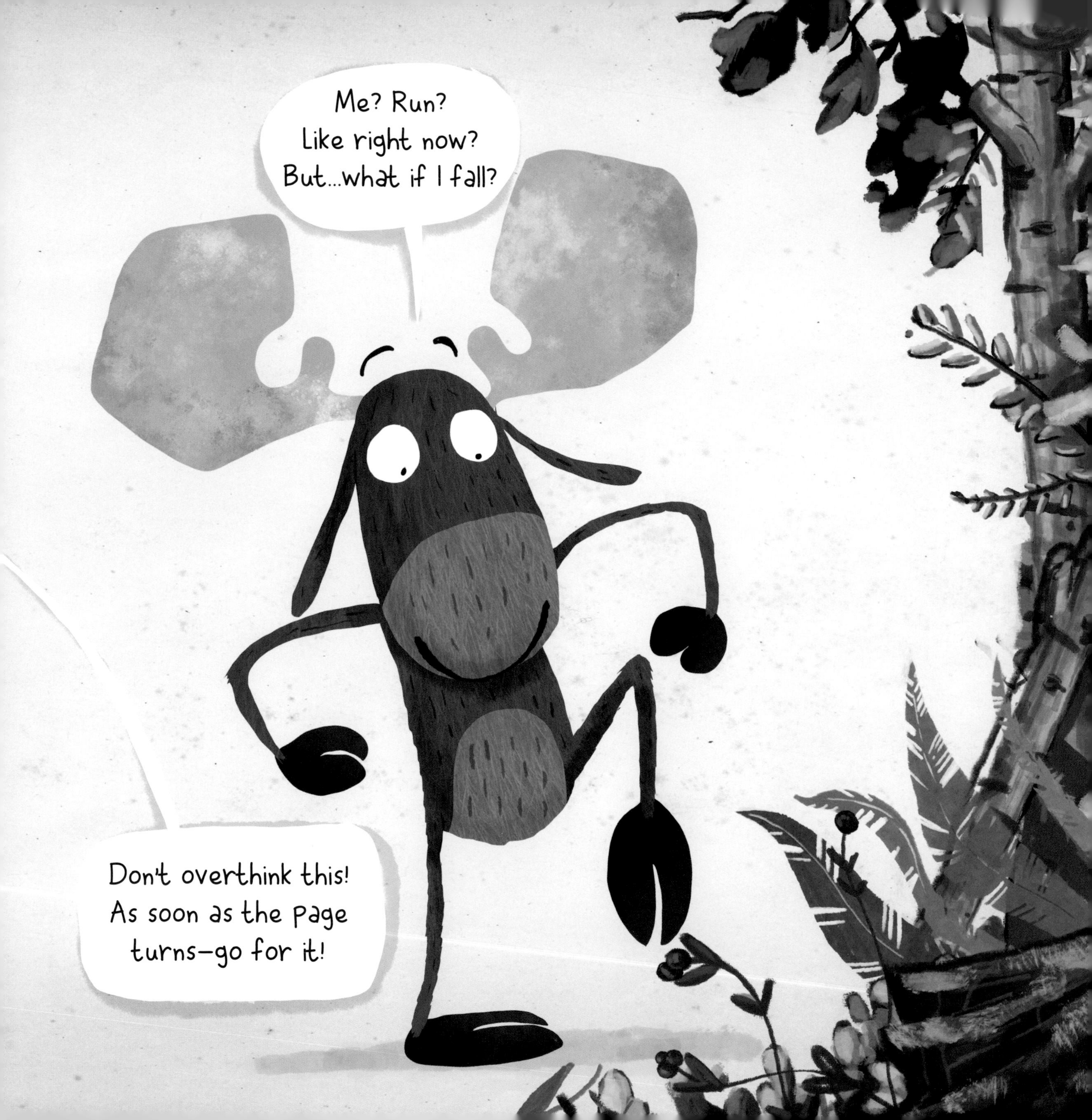
Me? Run? Like right now? But...what if I fall?
Don't overthink this! As soon as the page turns—go for it!

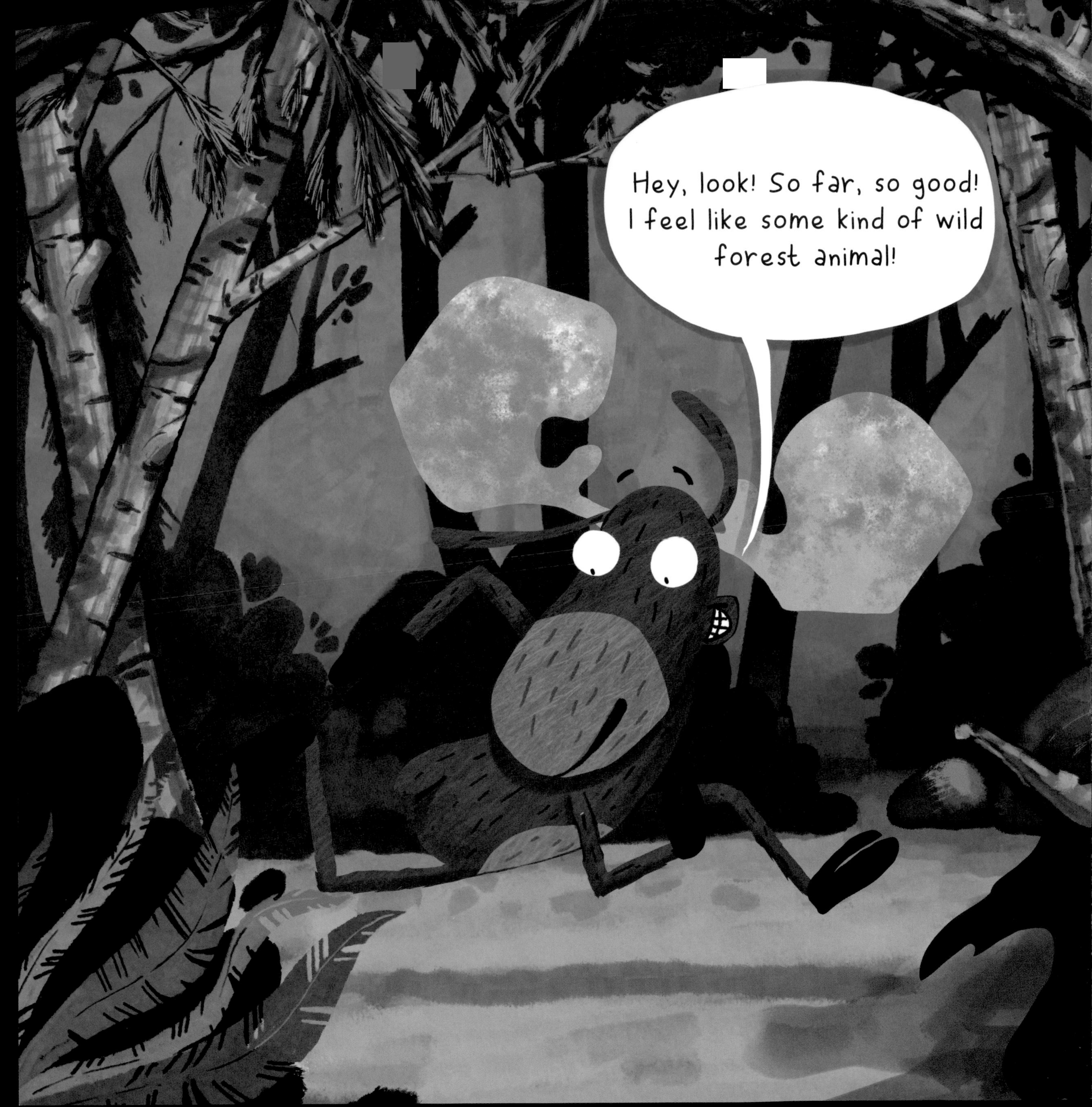
Hey, look! So far, so good! I feel like some kind of wild forest animal!

Moose have long legs, which are great for leaping over obstacles in the forest.

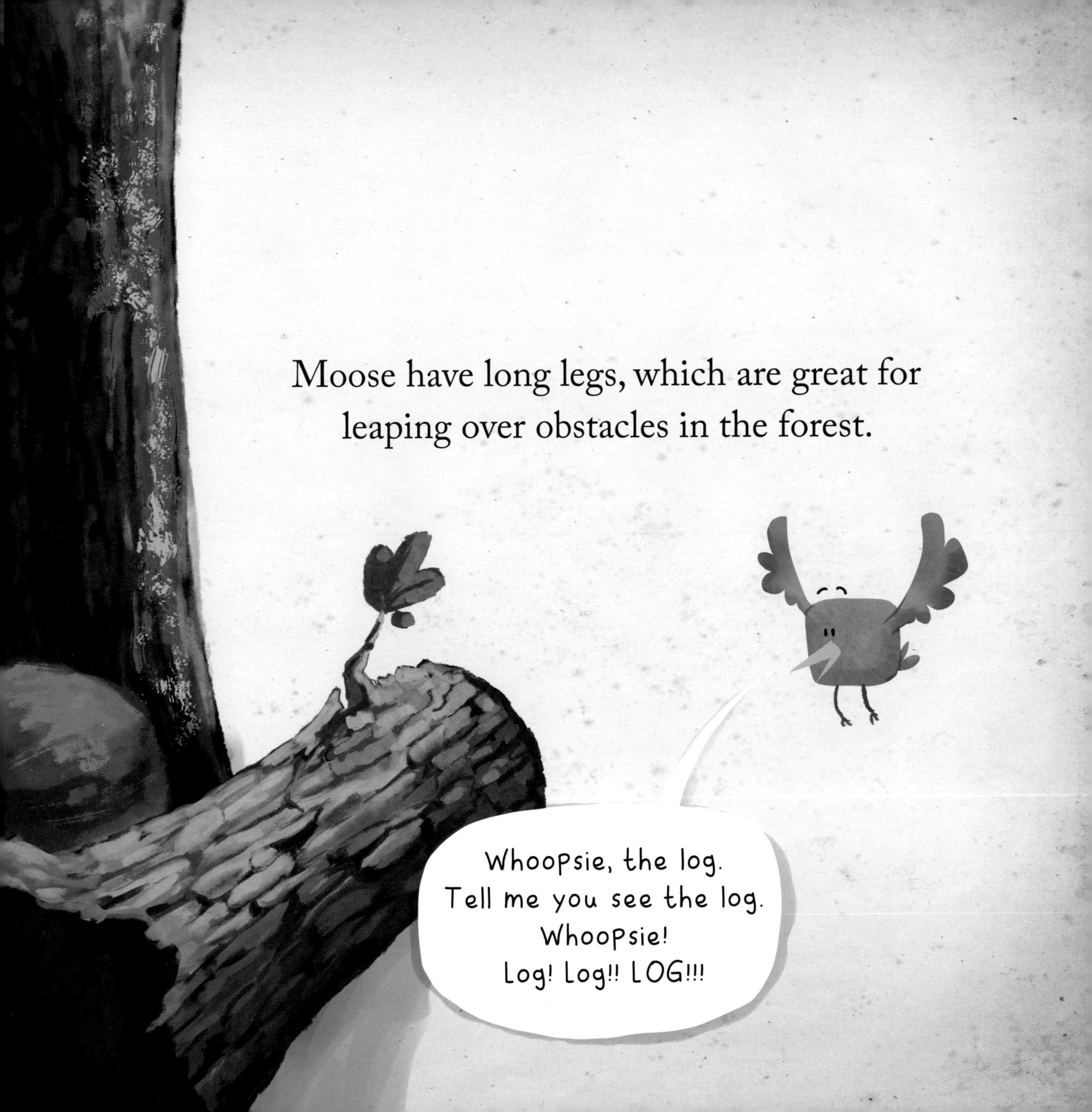
Whoopsie, the log.
Tell me you see the log.
Whoopsie!
Log! Log!! LOG!!!

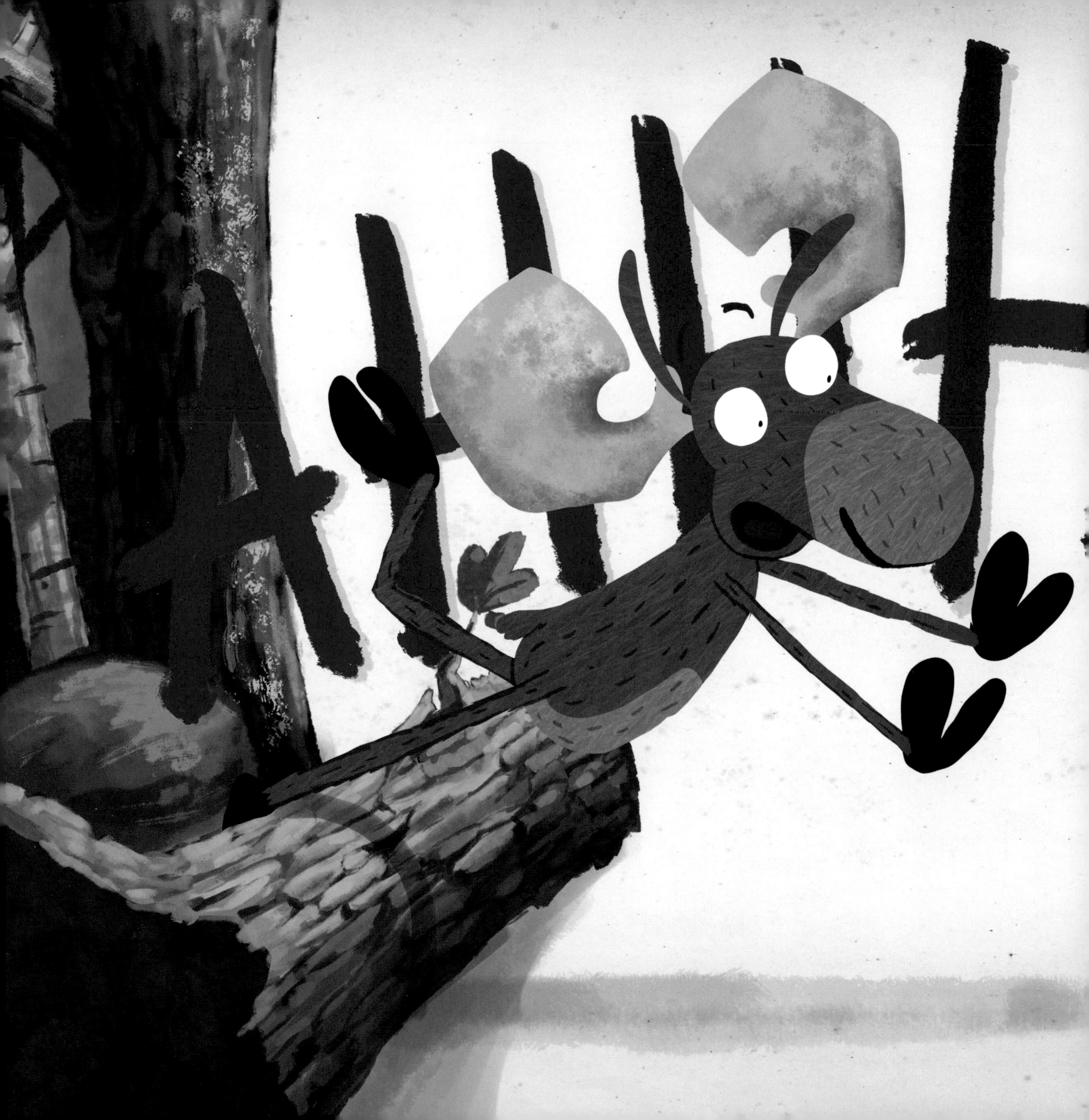

Mo have whic are great
ping o obstacles e fore

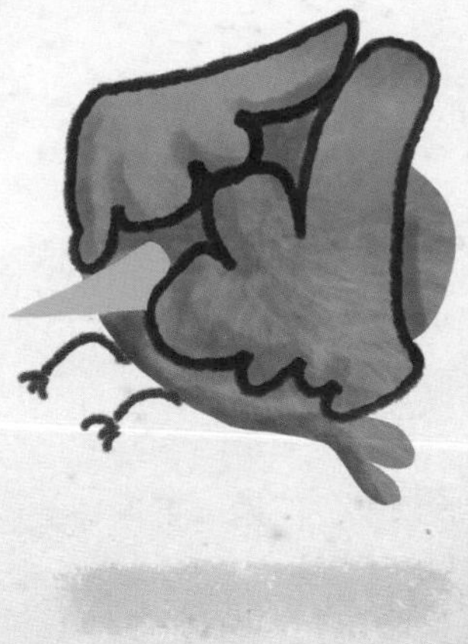

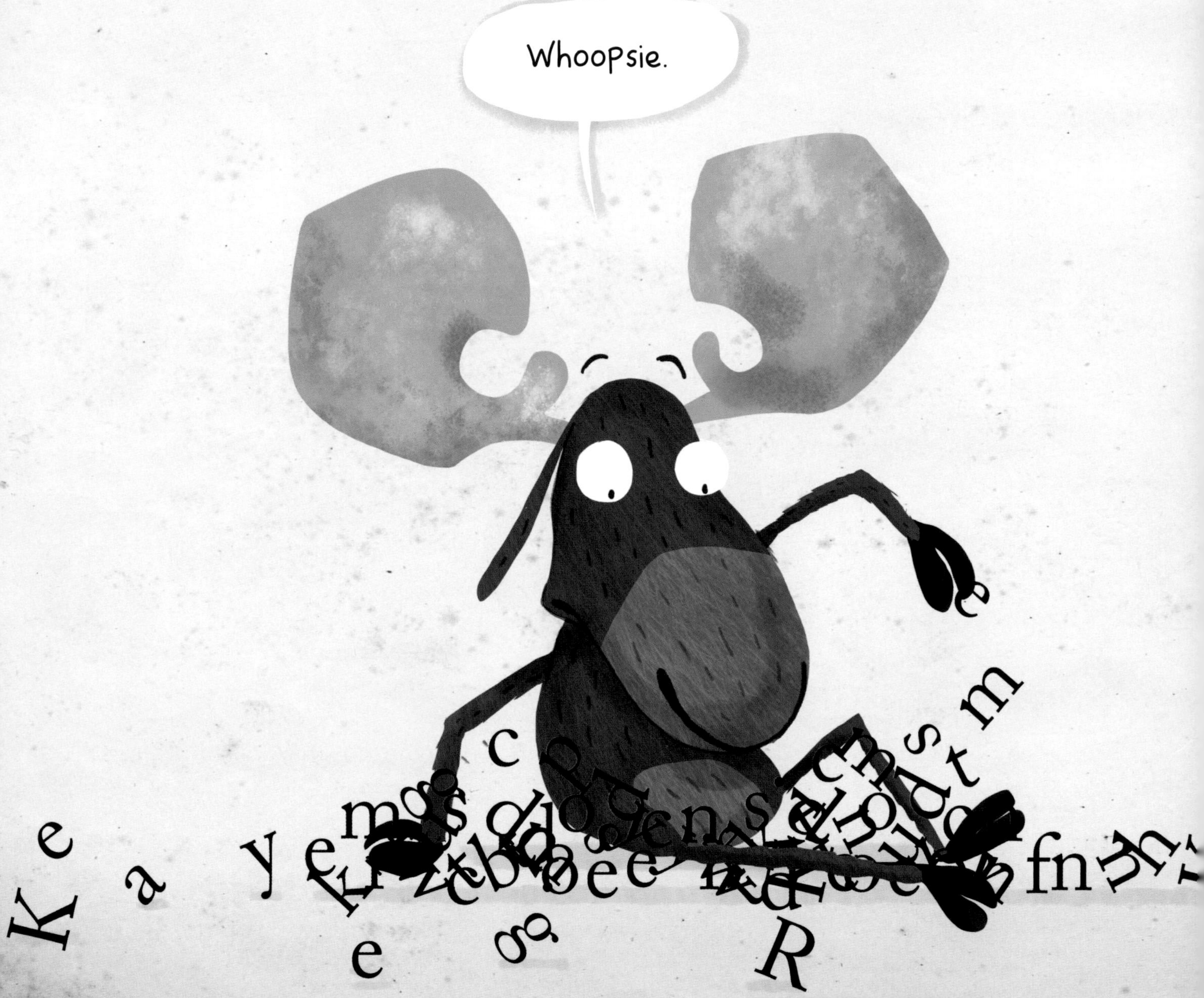
Whoopsie.

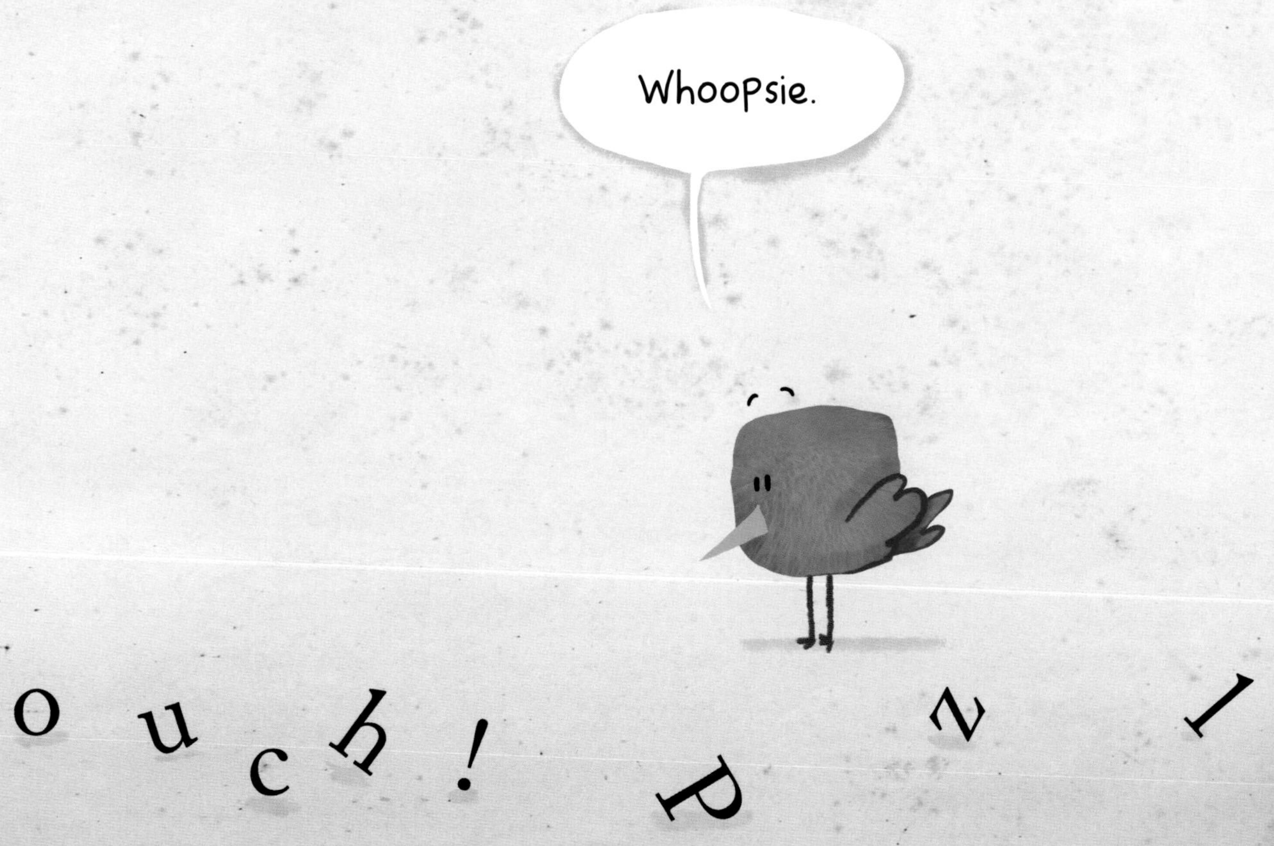
Whoopsie.
ouch! P z l

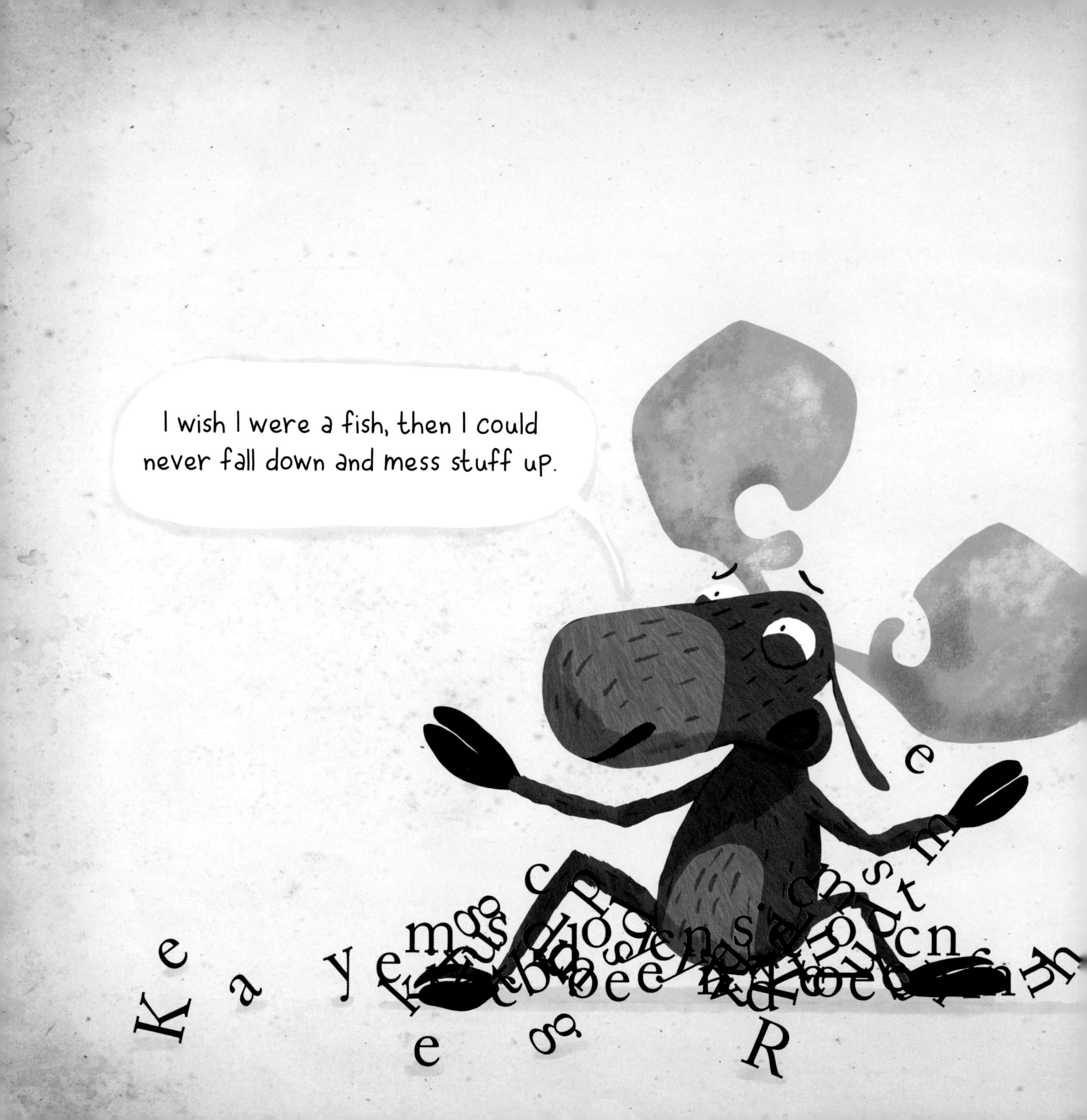
I wish I were a fish, then I could never fall down and mess stuff up.

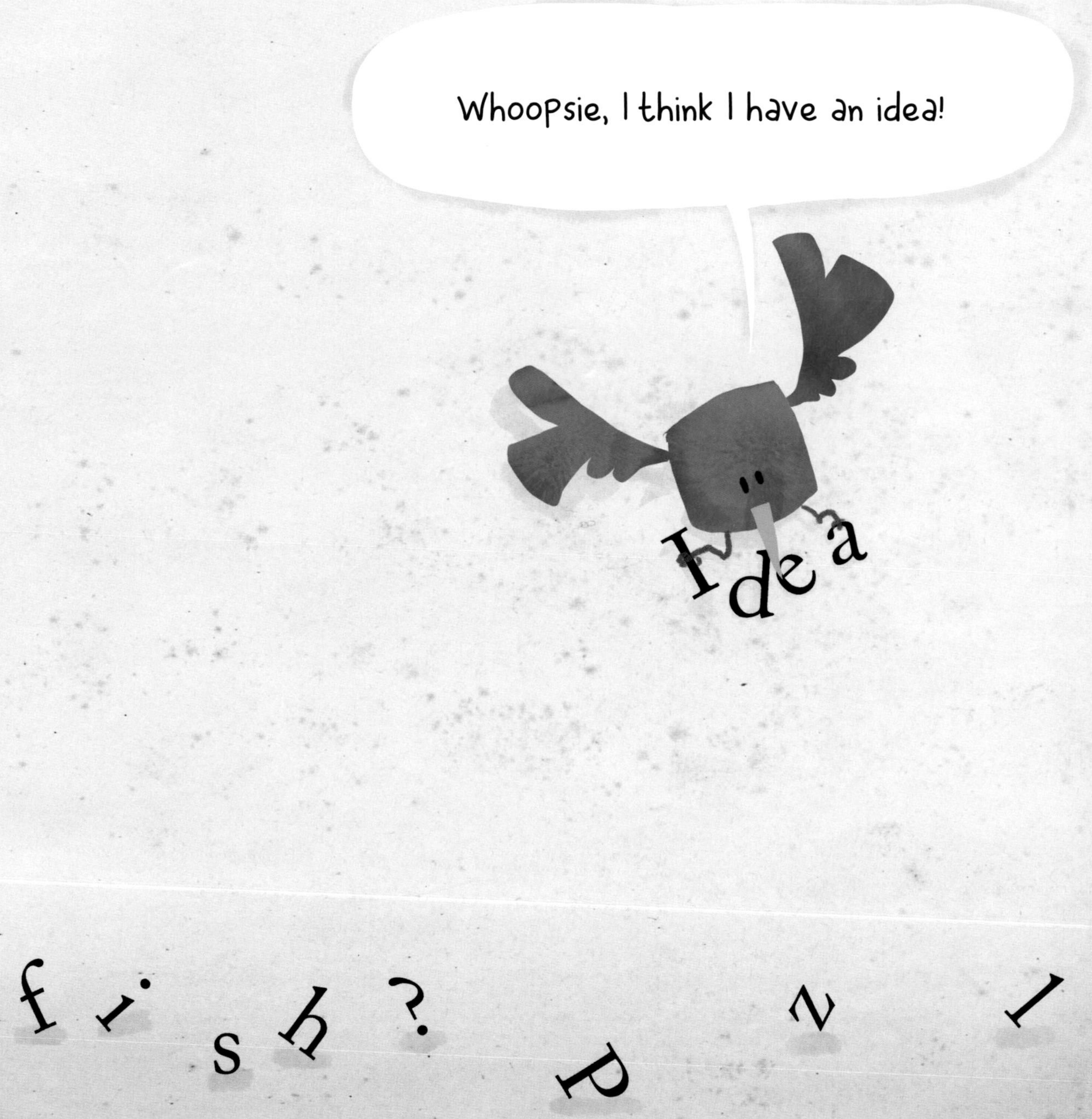

Whoopsie, I think I have an idea!
Idea
fish?
P z l

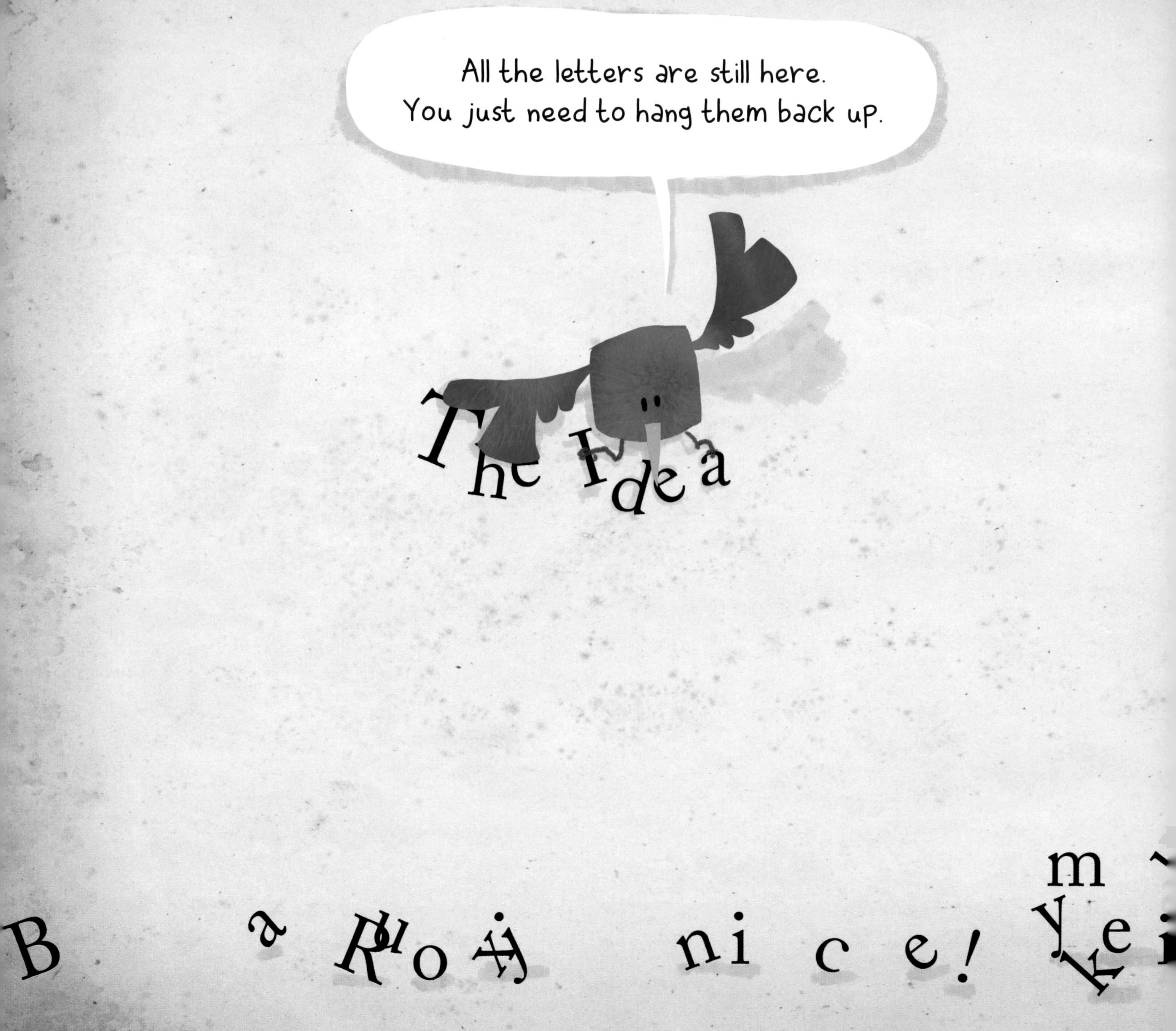
All the letters are still here.
You just need to hang them back up.
The Idea

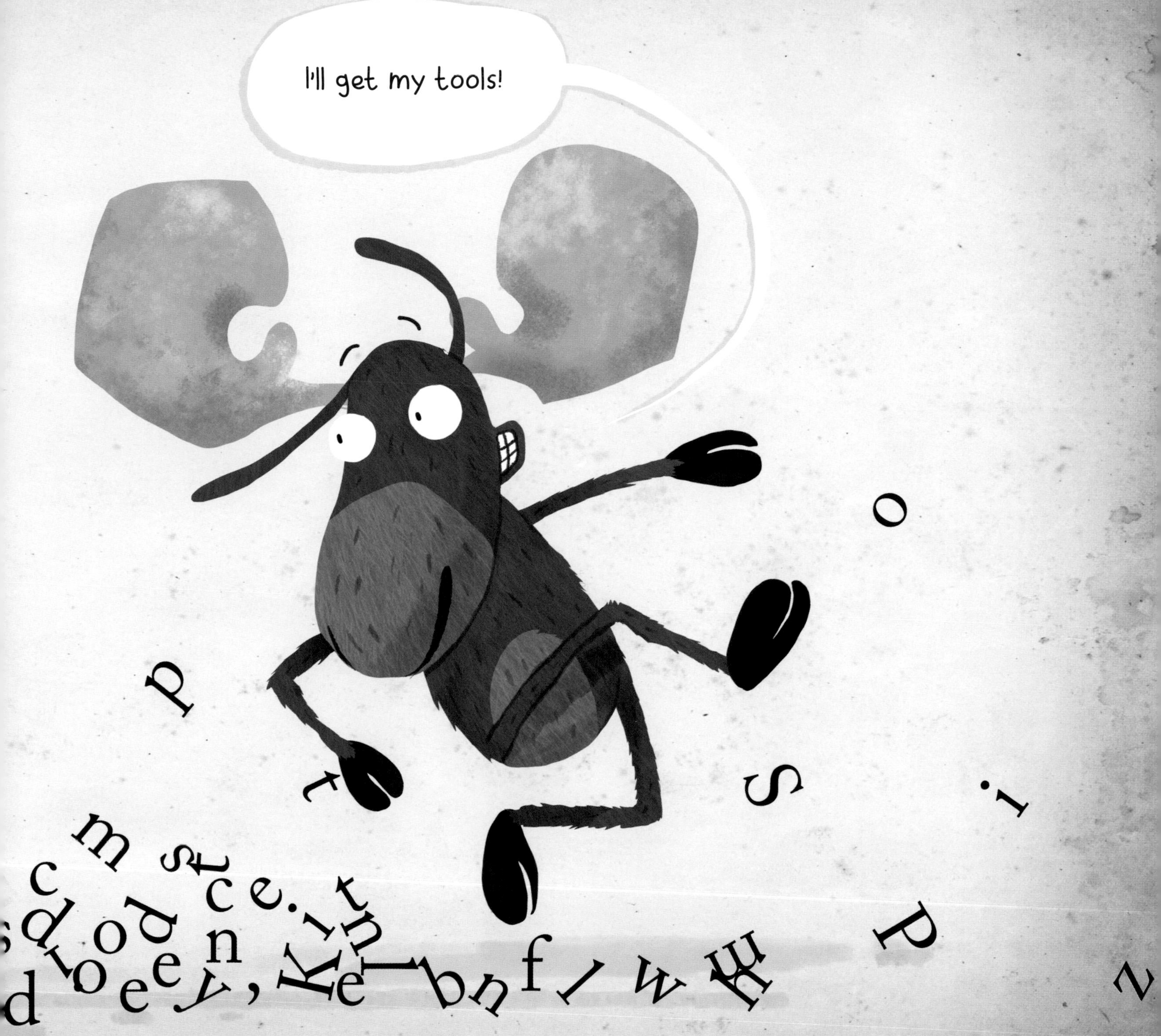
I'll get my tools!

Moose wear wild wigs
and laugh all night with
trampoline hamsters.

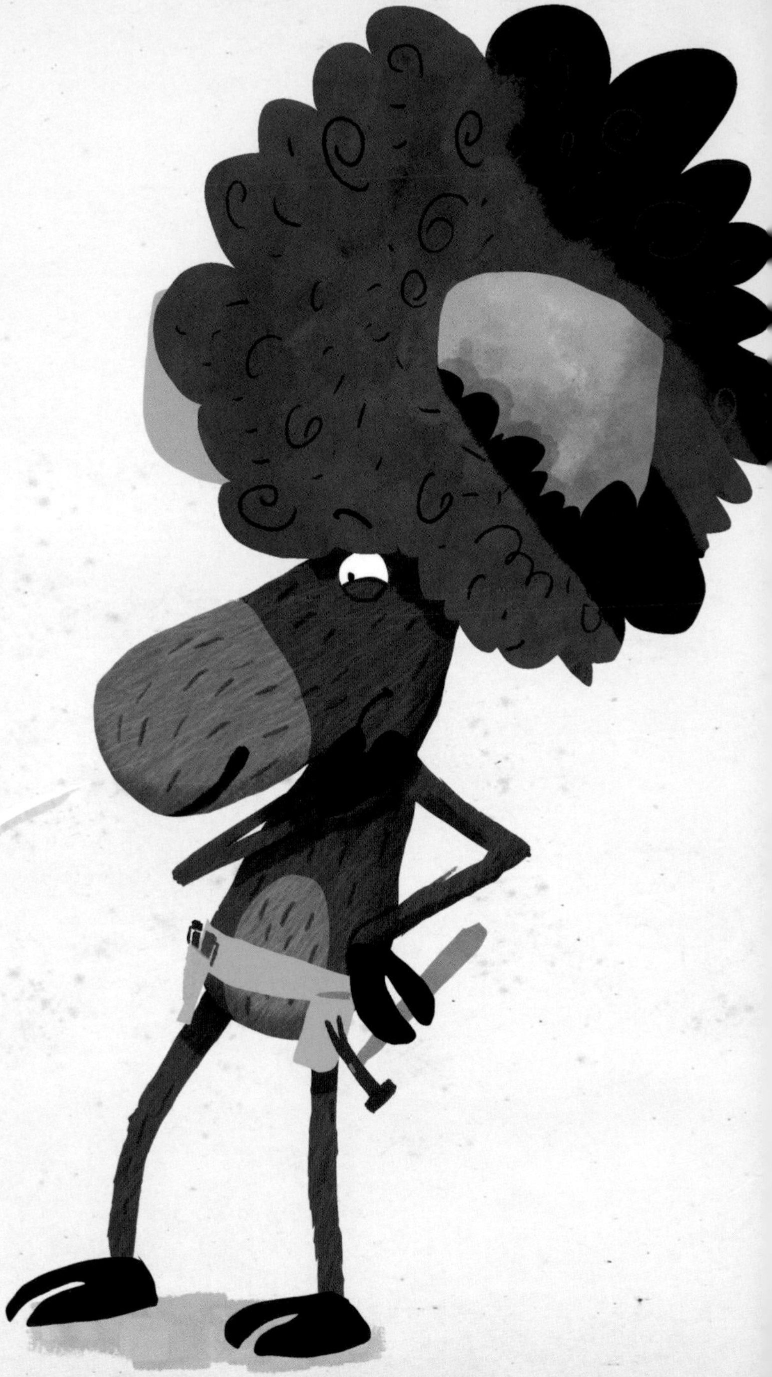

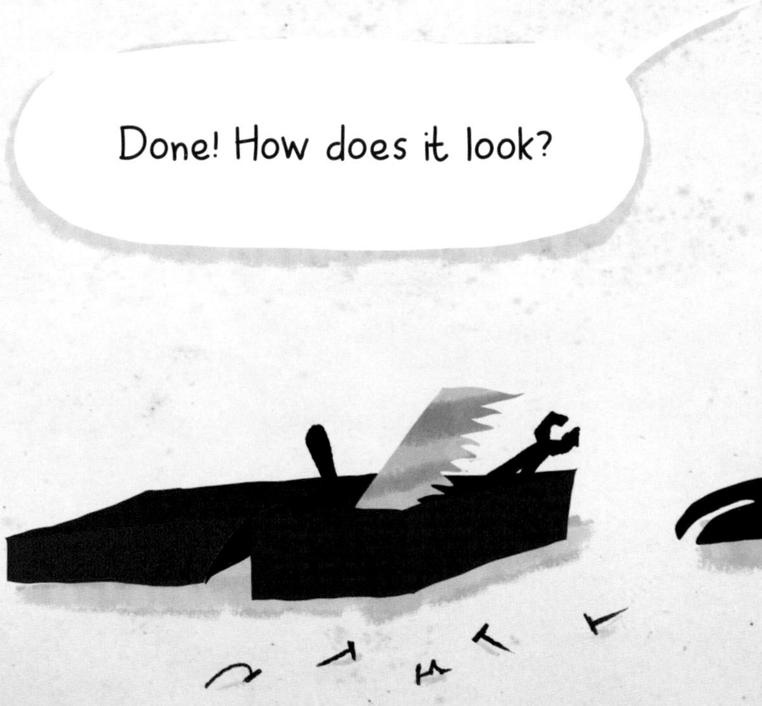
Done! How does it look?

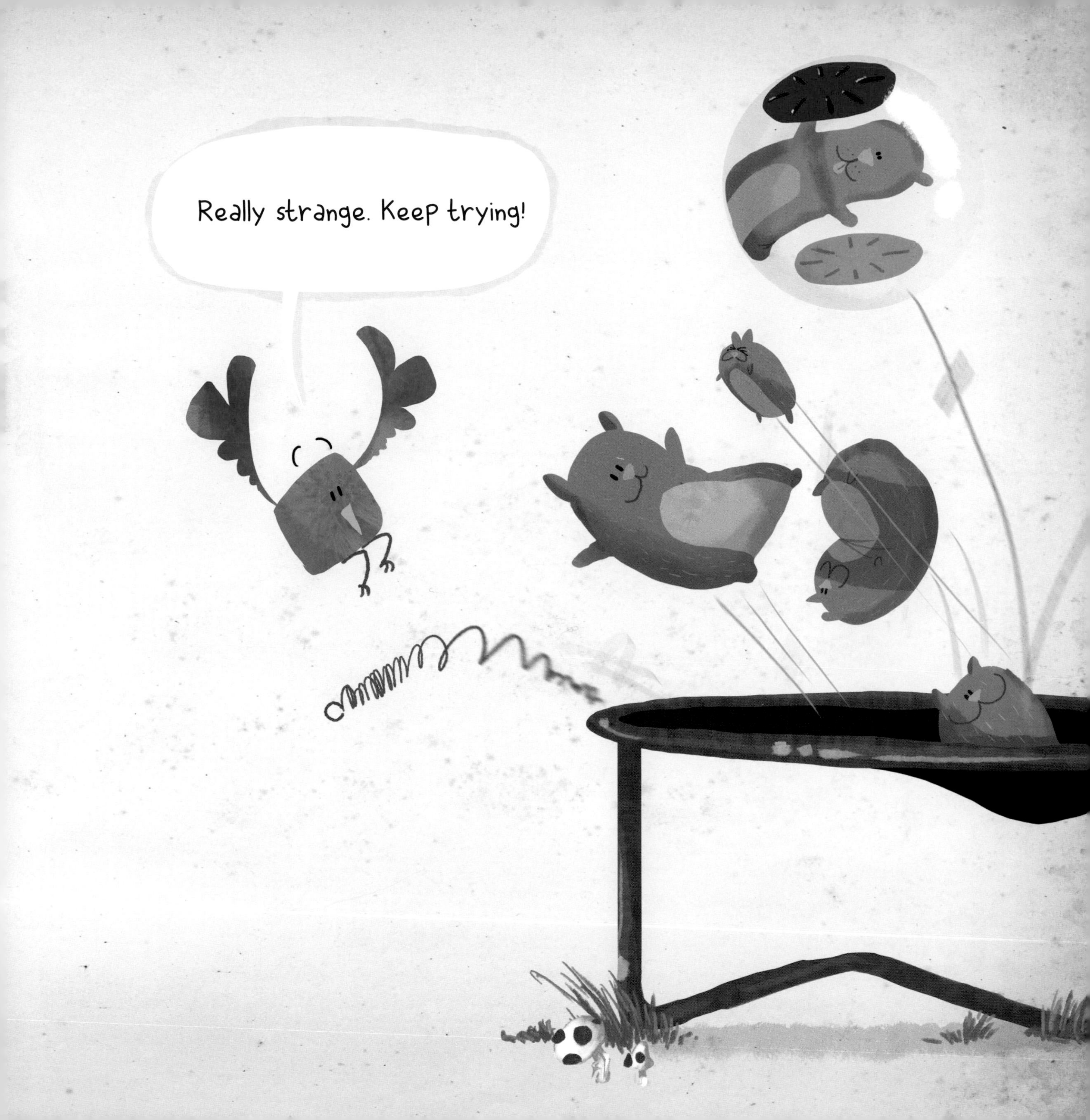
Really strange. Keep trying!

Mustached moose love line dancing with bears in fake beards.

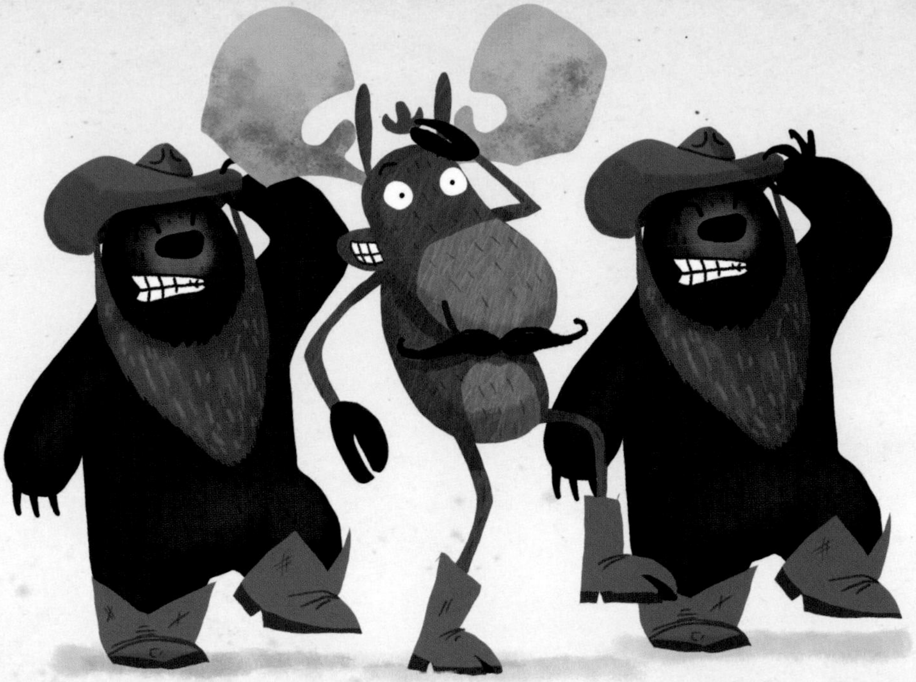

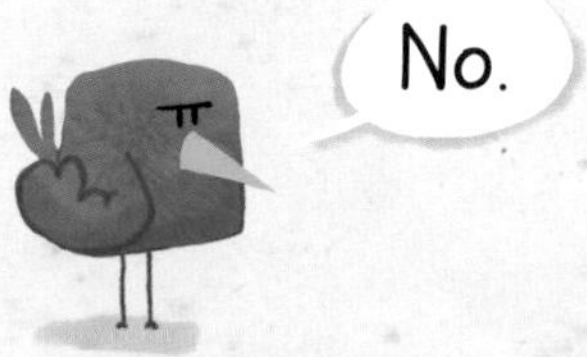
No.

Moose sing opera like dramatic donkey dudes.

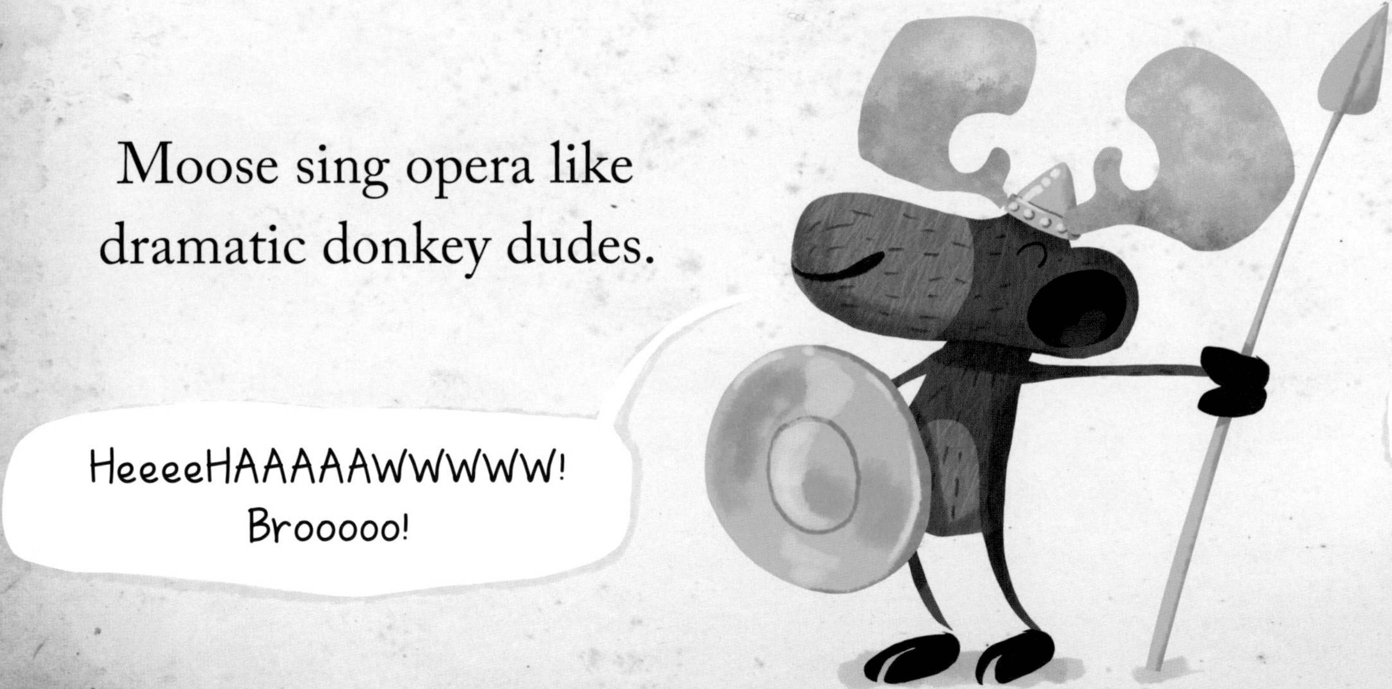
HeeeeHAAAAAWWWWW!
Broooooo!

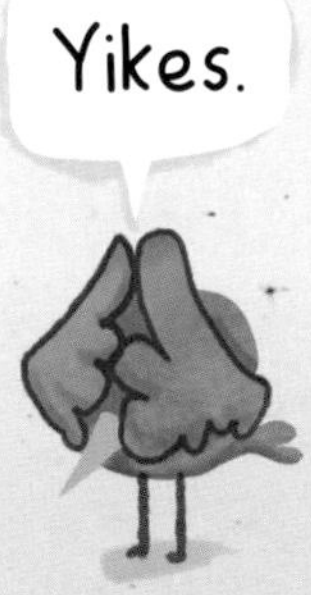
Yikes.

Moose have a thick coat of hare,
which keeps them warm year-round.

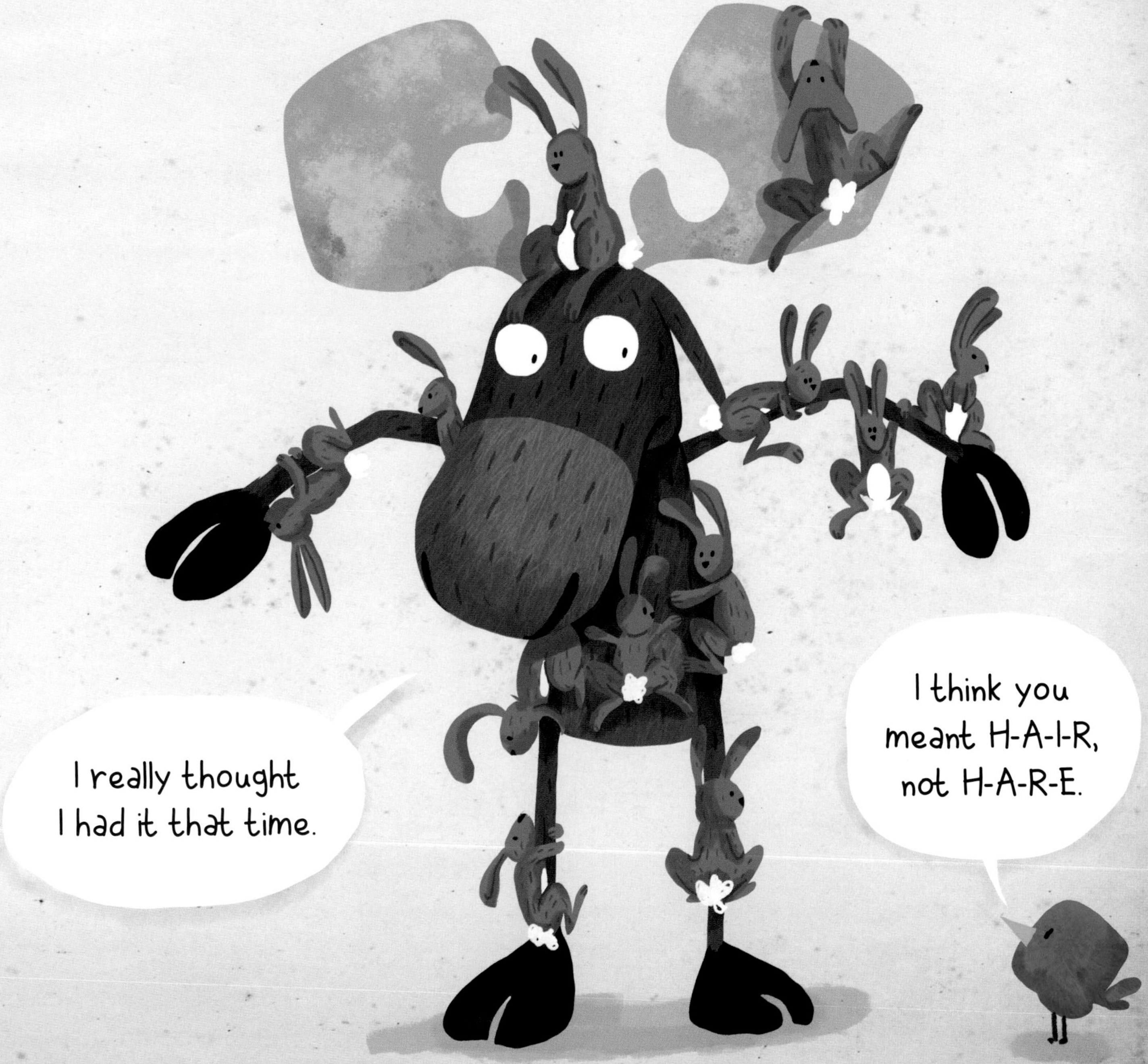
I really thought I had it that time.
I think you meant H-A-I-R, not H-A-R-E.

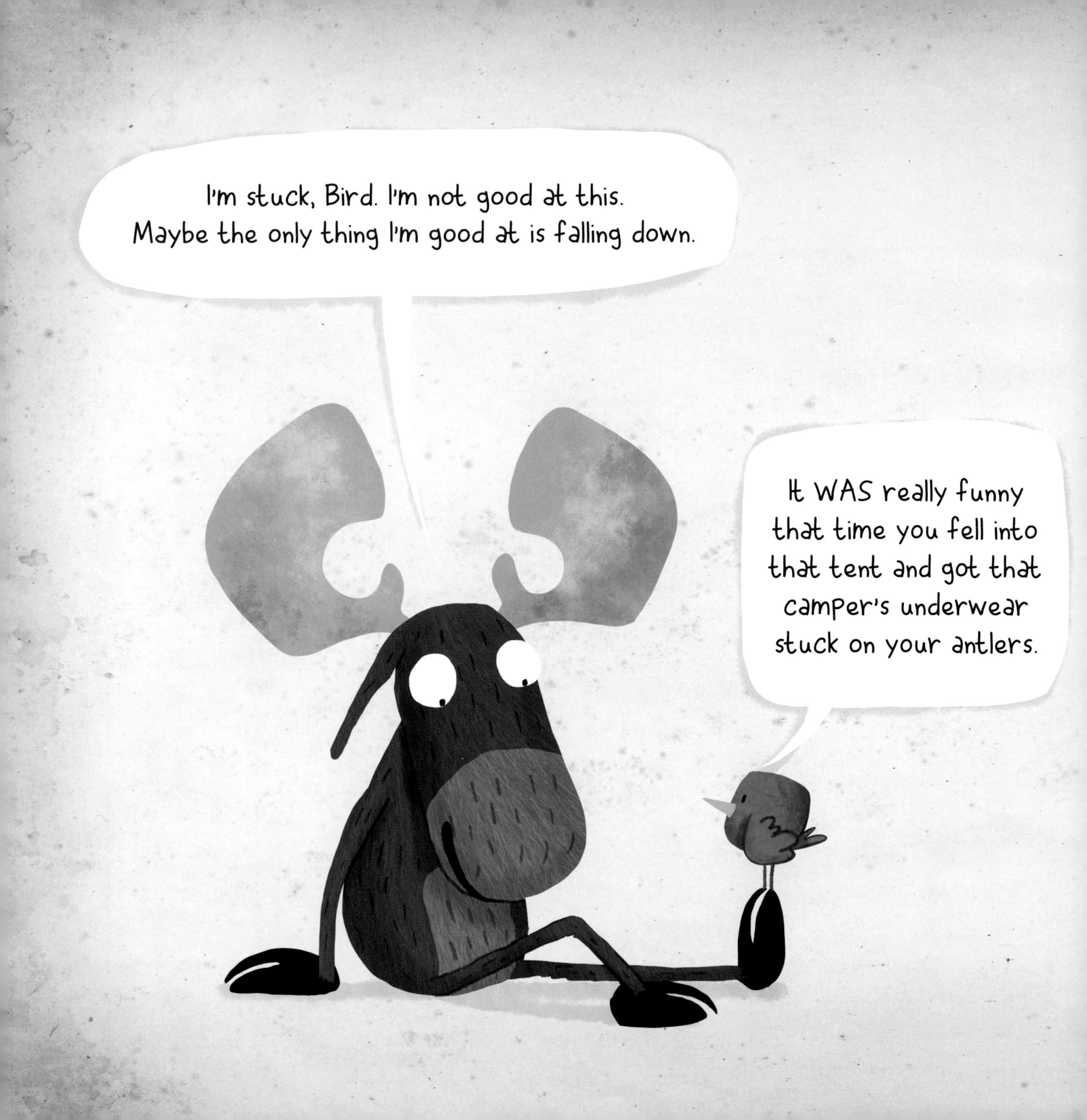
I'm stuck, Bird. I'm not good at this. Maybe the only thing I'm good at is falling down.
It WAS really funny that time you fell into that tent and got that camper's underwear stuck on your antlers.

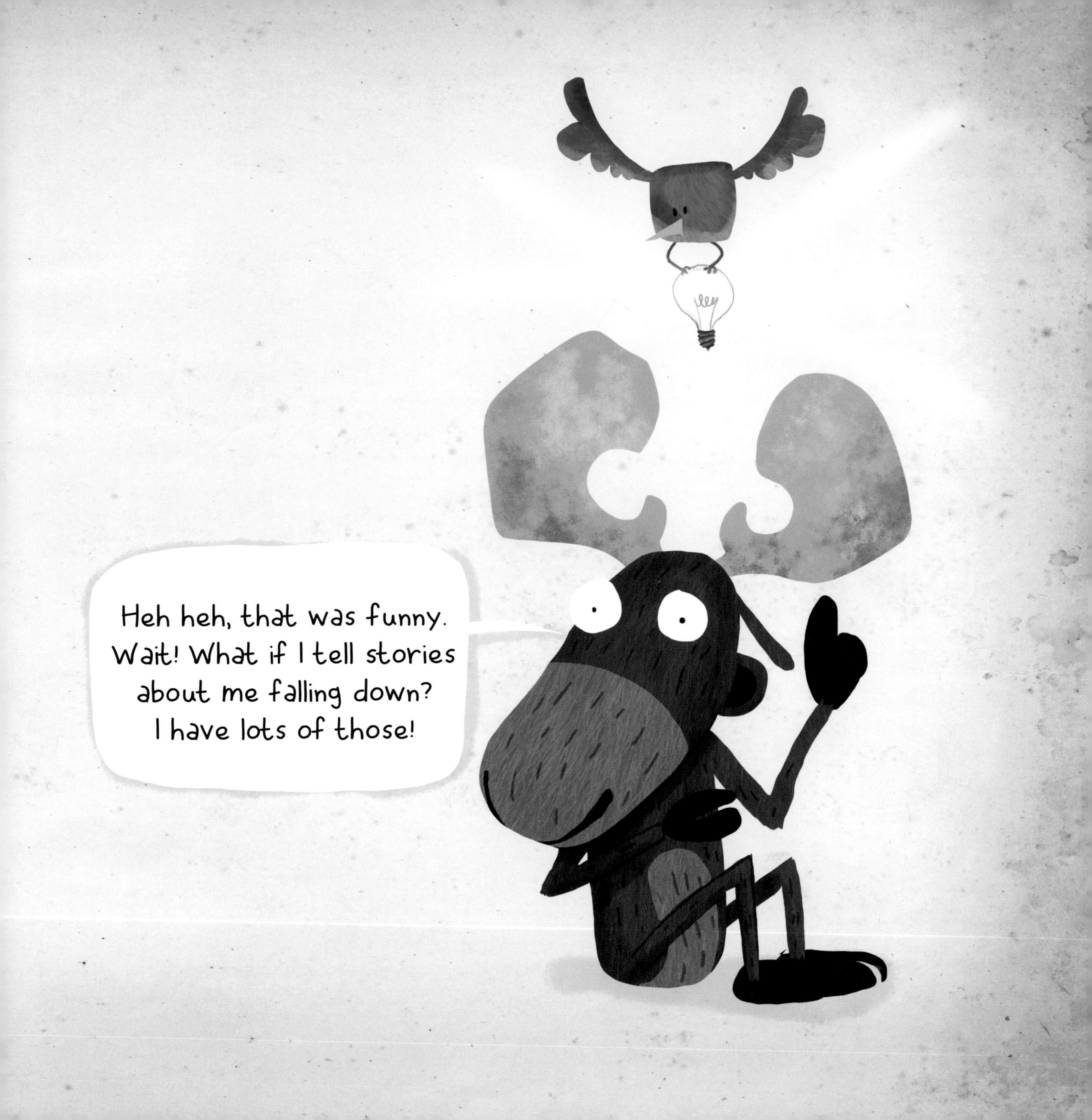
Heh heh, that was funny. Wait! What if I tell stories about me falling down? I have lots of those!

This moose has accidentally photobombed dozens of unsuspecting campers by falling into their pictures.

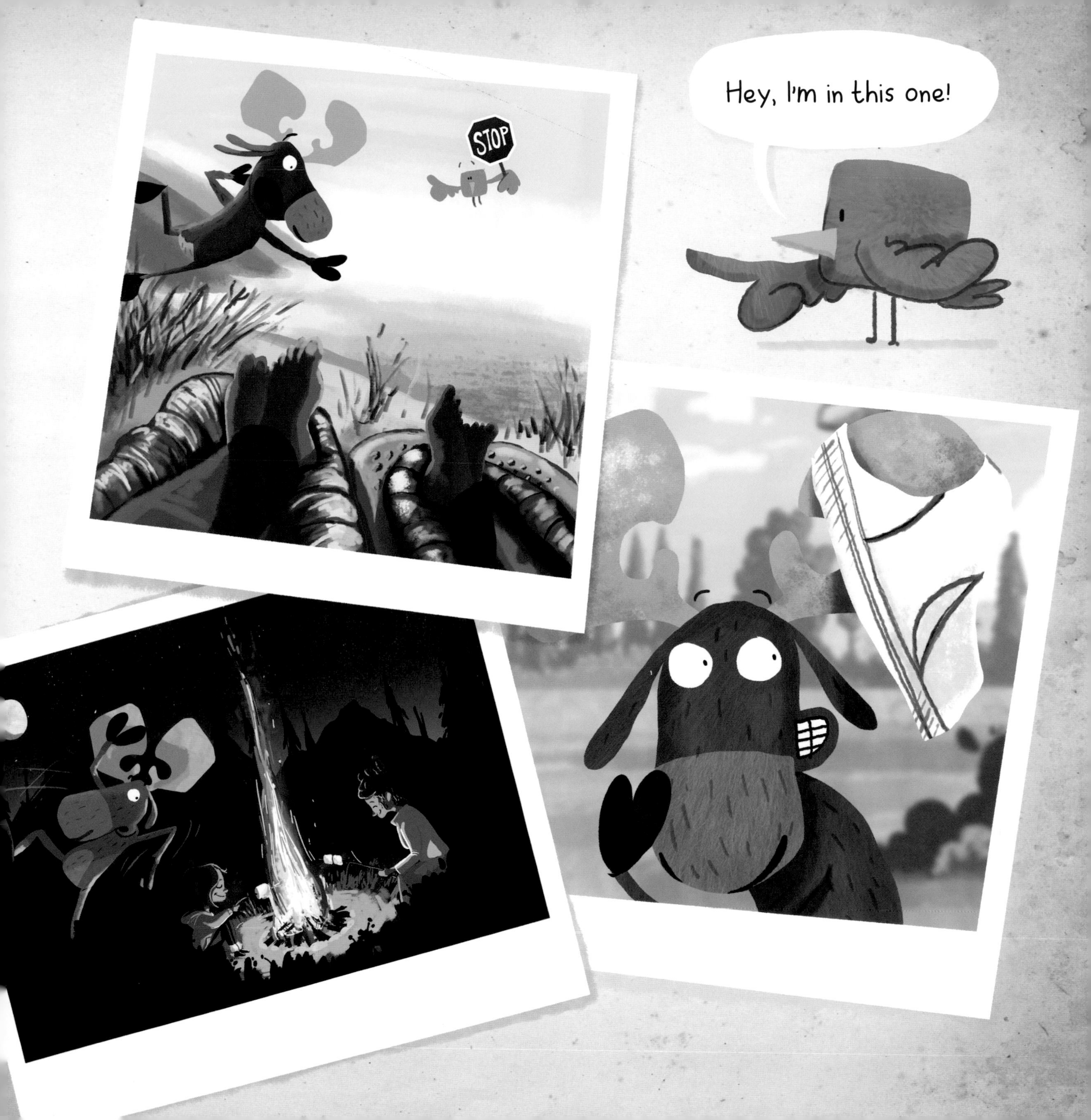
STOP
Hey, I'm in this one!

This moose owns the record for longest recorded fall UP a hill.

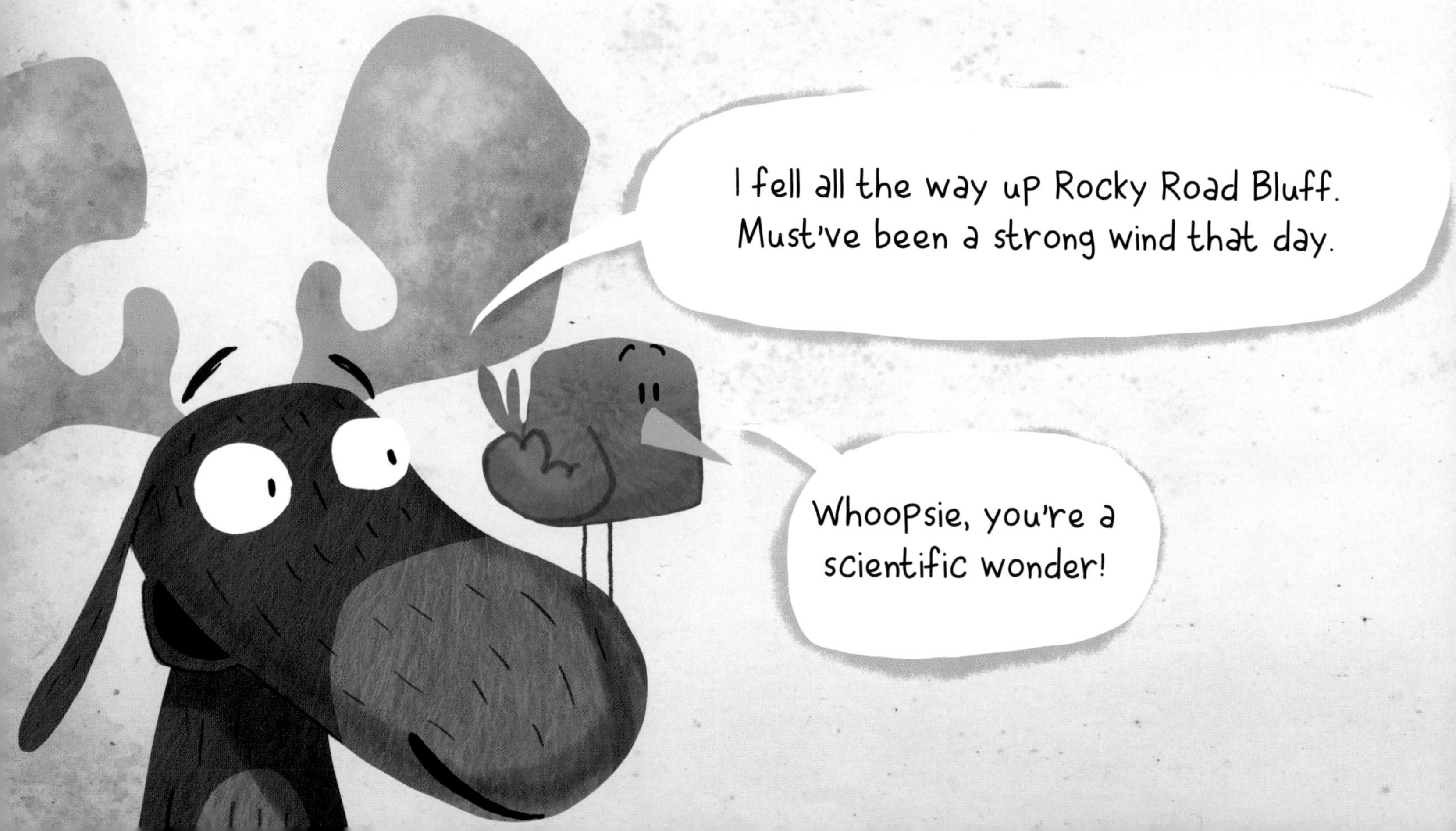
I fell all the way up Rocky Road Bluff. Must've been a strong wind that day.
Whoopsie, you're a scientific wonder!

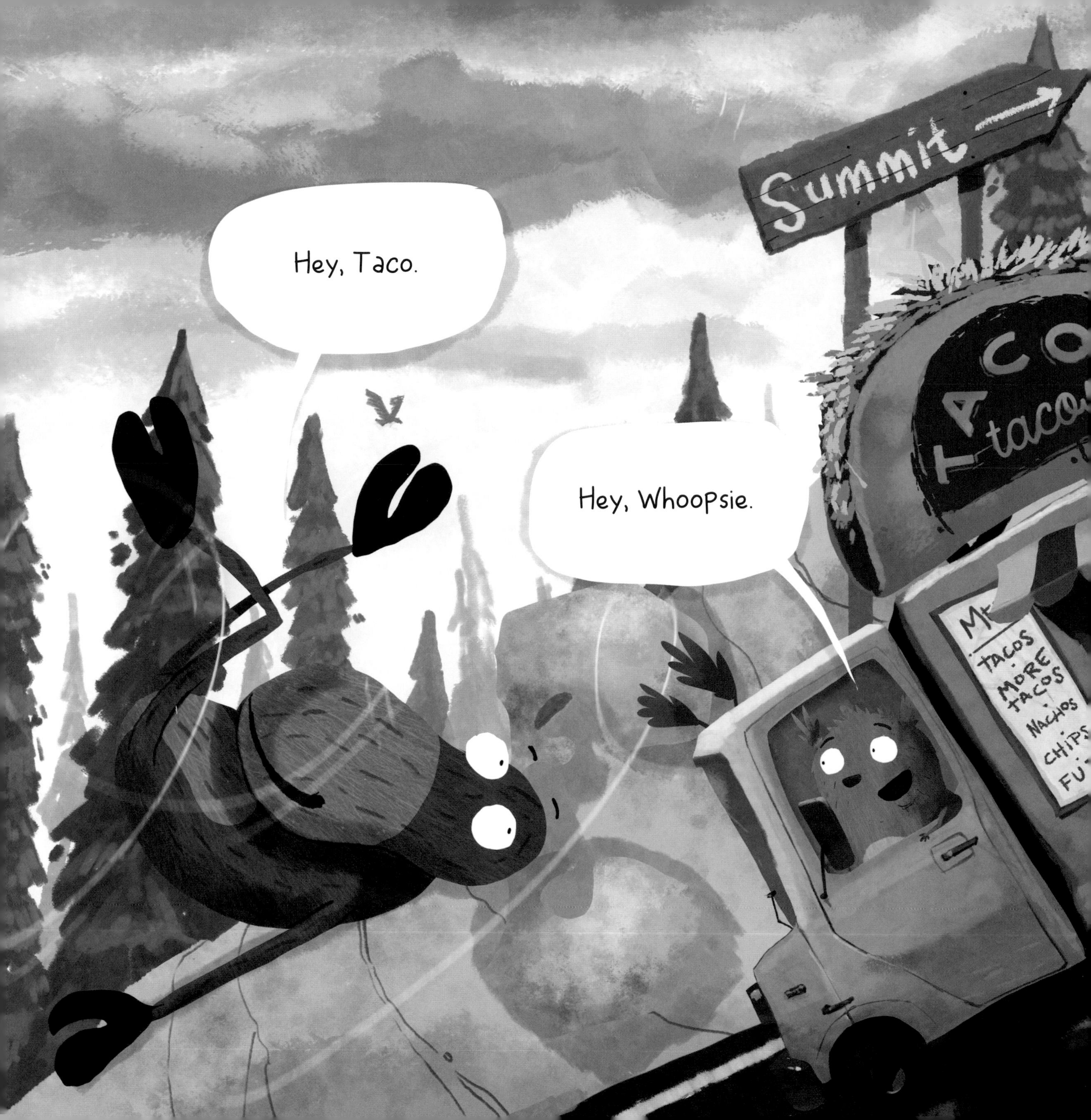
Hey, Taco.
Hey, Whoopsie.
Summit
TACOS
MORE TACOS
NACHOS

This moose even makes friends by falling.

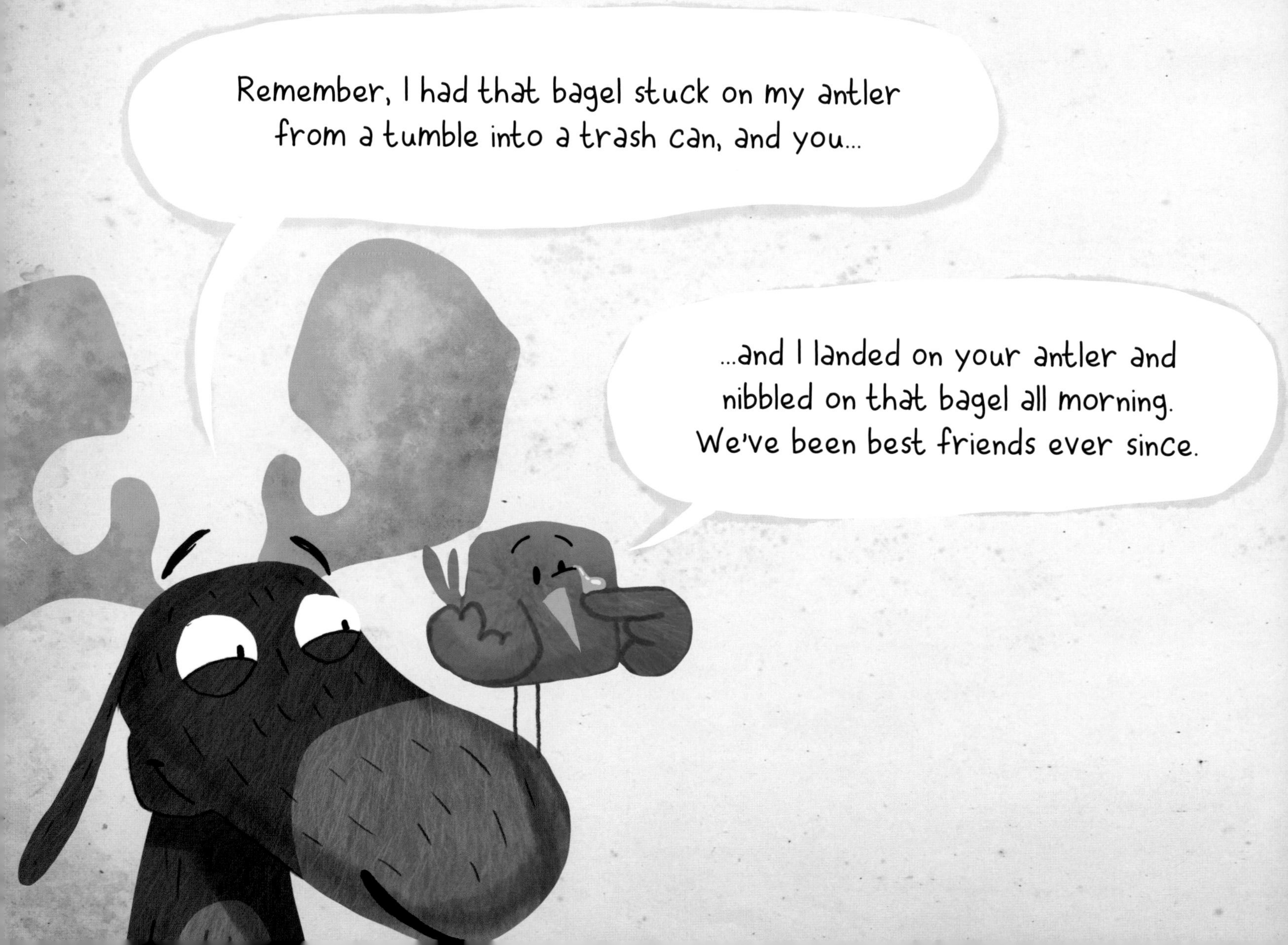
Remember, I had that bagel stuck on my antler from a tumble into a trash can, and you...
...and I landed on your antler and nibbled on that bagel all morning. We've been best friends ever since.

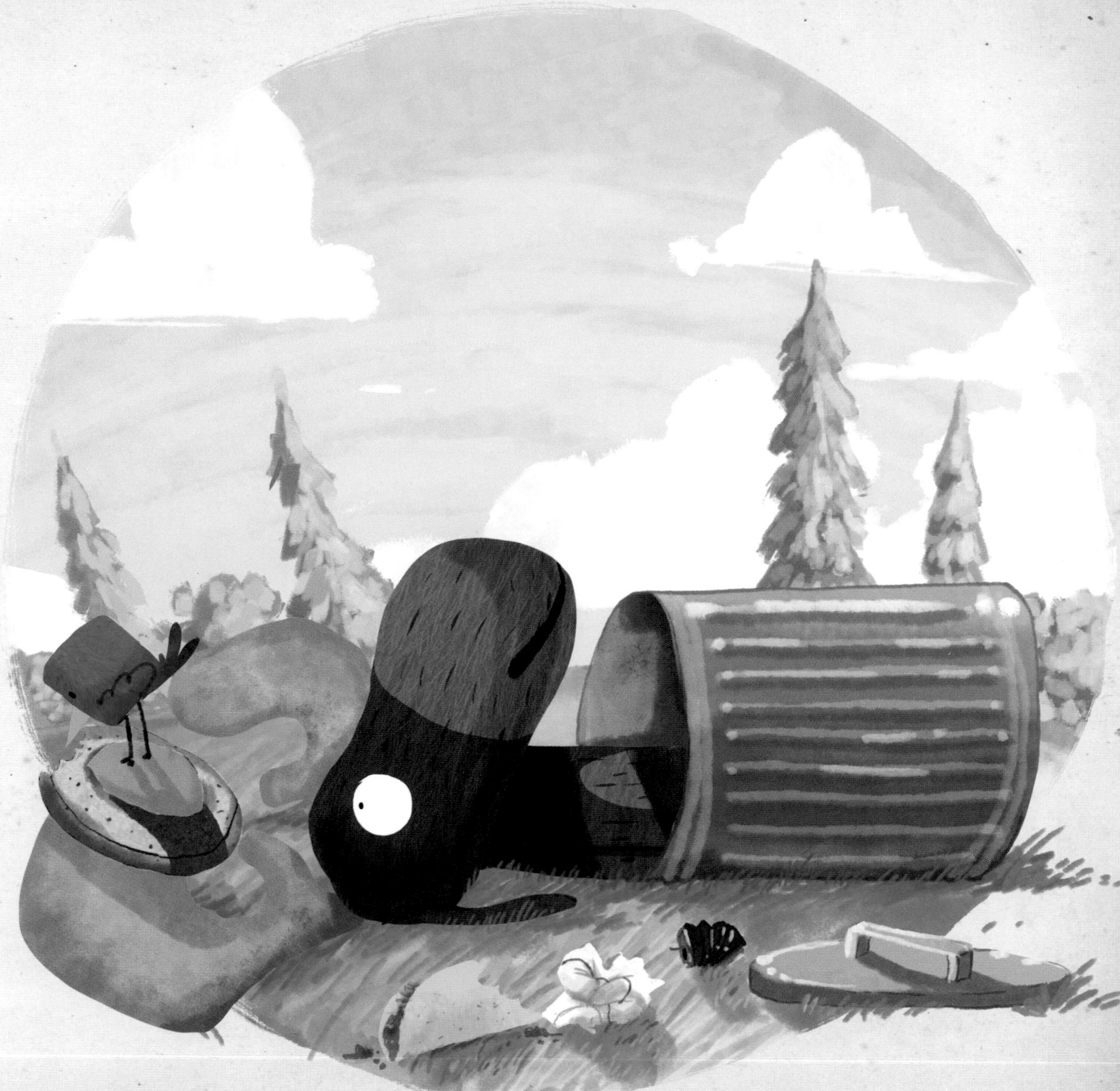

Yes, this moose is named "Whoopsie."
And he does fall down a lot.

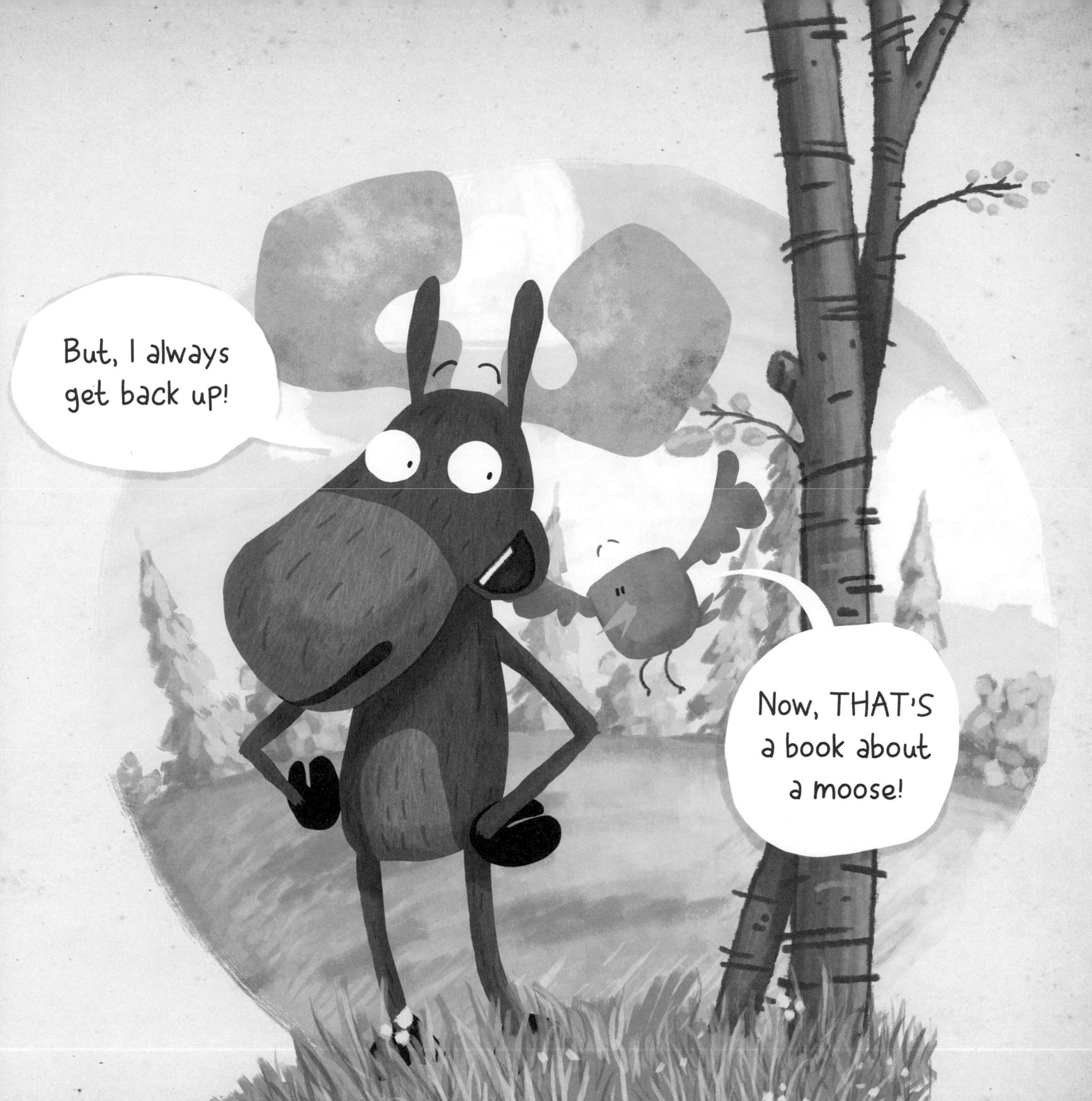
But, I always get back up!
Now, THAT'S a book about a moose!

ISBN: 978-1-941302-87-3

Library of Congress Control Number: 2018932767

www.lionforge.com

This Is a Whoopsie!, published 2018 by The Lion Forge, LLC. Copyright 2018 Josh Shipley and Andrew Cangelose. LION FORGE™ and CUBHOUSE™ and all associated distinctive designs are trademarks of The Lion Forge, LLC. All rights reserved. No similarity between any of the names, characters, persons, or institutions in this book with those of any living or dead person or institution is intended, and any such similarity which may exist is purely coincidental. Printed in China.

CUB™ HOUSE

10 9 8 7 6 5 4 3 2 1